The Hunter, the Hound and a Rogue

by Michael L. McCoy

with illustrations by Anisa L. Baucke

Book 3 in

The Chronicles of Peniel

published by

CHJ Publishing
1103 West Main
Middleton, Idaho, 83644

Text, cover and illustrations copyright © 2000
by Michael L. McCoy. All rights reserved.

Photographs on page 208 copyright © 2000
by Blaylock Photo Center. Used with permission.

Library of Congress Cataloging-in-Publication Data
00-132968

ISBN 0-927022-45-1

Printed in the United States of America

Acknowledgments

All thanks and praise to God Who provides me with talented and committed people who have worked to get this book published. Judy continues to be a helpmate who poured over the manuscript and offered suggestions regarding form and wise counsel concerning content. Once again the dedicated people at CHJ Publishing have been patient with me as they proposed suggestions and assisted in getting this work published. There are also those who have read the other books in this series and have encouraged me to continue adding to the number in print.

Soli Deo Gloria!

To the Reader and the Hearer

G. K. Chesterton wrote that "the story-tellers do not merely exist to tell the stories; the stories exist to tell us something about the story-tellers." This is most certainly true in general and particularly so with this book. However, to keep the focus directed on the main Character intended by the author, let the reader and the hearer know that this story-teller does not merely write to tell a story; this story is written to tell you something about the Story-teller.

Michael L. McCoy
Ash Wednesday
8 March Anno Domini 2000

TABLE OF CONTENTS

1	Summer Vacation	7
2	A Frail, Old Man	13
3	First Echo	20
4	Infant Nightmare	27
5	The Other	34
6	On the Run	42
7	Pursued	47
8	Return to the Holy Place	54
9	No One's Here	62
10	Moonlight Tears	69
11	Friends in Battle	79
12	A Baby's Protection	86
13	The Final Blow	94
14	The Proclamation	99
15	Two Conversations	107
16	Watcher and Watched	116
17	Someone's Wagon is Fixed	120
18	Shared Love	128
19	Harvest Sought, Prey Caught	137
20	Ah Yes!	147
21	Family	150
22	Life Searching and Soul Searching	157
23	Wisdom from of Old	164
24	Possibilities	171
25	The Steadfast Promise of the Word	178
26	No Returning	184
27	Rebuilding	189
28	An Autumn Sunset	192
29	Wrestling	199
30	The Continuing Story	204

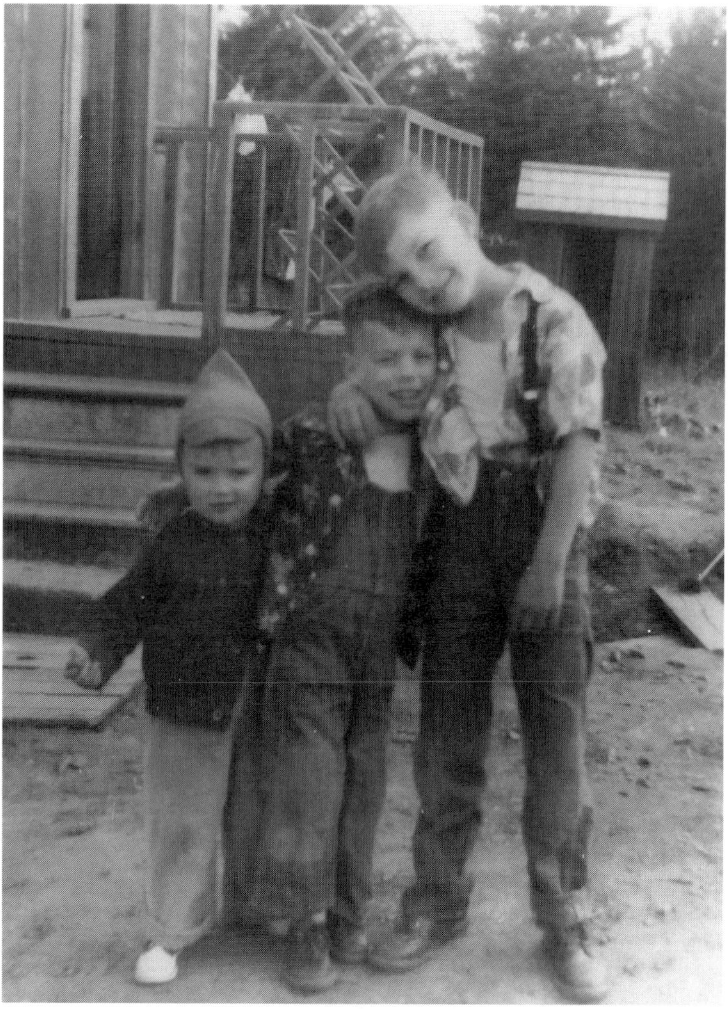

CHAPTER 1

SUMMER VACATION

Near the end of summer vacation, a grandma and grandpa invited their grandchildren to stay with them for two weeks. The grandma sent an invitation to each of the five children. Because these children loved being with their grandparents and since this fortnight would be just prior to the start of the school year, the children gladly and quickly accepted grandma's invitation. (Their parents were just as glad because summer had long since become quite boring to the children.) The youngest grandchild, a seven year-old boy named Mick, thought a flood might keep them from returning home and beginning school.

The children lived two states and 400 miles from grandma and grandpa, and as a result, the grandchildren did not have many opportunities to visit. Mick remembered that Grampa always wore khaki-colored clothes, had a tan baseball cap and always worked in his wood shop. He thought that Grampa smelled a lot like sawdust. Kay was the youngest granddaughter and on previous visits in the winter, she helped grandma by carrying wood for the fireplace.

In addition, she always wanted to wear one of grandma's aprons and do some cooking with her. At night, Ellen liked to sleep in the upper room where the ceiling sloped because of the roof. She enjoyed being by herself in the bed and listening to the grownups talking downstairs. She heard their voices but could not always make out what they were saying. Sometimes she smiled in the dark when she heard grandma laugh.

Chris and Gerrie were identical twins and had been teenagers for nearly a year. They were the oldest of the grandchildren. One of their favorite activities was exchanging clothes several times a day and pretending to be each other. The only way anyone could tell them apart was that one of them had a birthmark on the top of her head. There was a small spot where no hair grew. (In all honesty, I can not remember which one of them had this birthmark.)

Anyway, the three younger children arrived first. Ellen, after hugging and kissing her grandparents, asked grandma if she could sleep in the upper room with the sloped ceiling. Grandma's smile indicated that the room awaited Ellen's presence. She told her, "The bed's just waitin' for you to run up and plop down on it." (Grandma talked that way. It was one of the many things that made her special to her grandchildren.) Ellen ran up the two flights of stairs and put her bag on the bed. She found a note on the pillow, "This is Ellen's bed." She said to herself, "Perfect; away from the others and in my own place. She was a quiet girl who, at times, liked to be by herself to read and twirl her hair around her finger as she explored a book. As she smiled and fell back onto the bed, she rediscovered the water stain on the ceiling tile above her head. Last winter Ellen decided the shape resembled a friendly forest troll with lime green moss growing on its back.

Mick gave grandma a quick hug and told her that he loved her. After she let go of him, he ran to grandpa and jumped into his arms. Mick inhaled deeply so his first breathe in grandpa's lap was filled with the aroma of sawdust. The boy closed his eyes and he was taken back to his childhood once more.

"Grampa, I love you!"

"I love you, too, Mick. It's so good to have you here with us. It's been too long, more than six months since you left here the last time. You've grown so much."

"Yea, I'm a whole bunch older than before when I was just a little kid."

"Come with me. I'll show you where you'll be sleeping. We never had all five of you kids here at one time, so we had to do a little rearranging. I picked the spot for you, but you don't have to sleep in it if you don't want to, okay?"

Grampa took him upstairs and into a large walk-in closet at the end of the hallway. In the closet a bed made from an old sleeping bag and a jeans quilt was on the floor in the corner. The bed took up more than half of the floor space. Mick thought it was the best, the perfect hideout. No robbers would ever think of looking in a closet.

Kay had kissed grandpa and let the others hug grandma first. She wanted to be last because she could hold onto her grandma for a long, long time. Three kisses and two lengthy hugs later, Kay whispered into grandma's ear, "Do you have an apron for me to wear?"

"I think you'll find one over there on the stool by the stove."

Kay skipped to it and tied it around her waist. The last time she had been at grandma's house, the apron she wore was adult size. The ties were wrapped under her armpits and tied in the back. Even so, she had to be careful not to trip herself by stepping on the bottom of the apron. Today she discovered the apron that grandma had given to her was just her size. Her eyes sparkled, she giggled and blurted out, "Let's get cooking, grandma!"

"We sure will. Go ahead and get your stuff put in the big bedroom at the top of the stairs."

Kay quickly did as she was told and returned to the kitchen to help grandma with a batch of homemade fudge. She used a long wooden spoon to make certain it didn't stick to the bottom. The spoon also was suitable for Kay's taste-testing. A half hour later the fudge was done and the twins arrived out front.

Chris and Gerrie, while short for their age, were filled with cleverness, spunk and mischief. Gerrie often devised cagey schemes that Chris carried out with a willing spirit. Chris, the unappointed adventurer, took Gerrie's plans and brought them to life. Gerrie followed and supported. An unspoken code of protection and silence existed between the sisters, even when others became suspicious. They fixed their hair so that the telltale spot remained hidden. At times the caper was quite simple and over in short order, like when they had school pictures taken and switched names. No one became suspicious or could detect anything out of the ordinary when the pictures arrived. (By the way, their parents still don't know about this switch.)

Other plans were carried out over a long period of time. When the twins were seven years-old, Gerrie thought it a spiffy idea to put some salt in the sugar bowl. As Gerrie stood lookout, Chris placed a little salt in the bowl. Their dad, the only one who used sugar in his coffee, began to complain about the bitter taste. Year after year, every once in a while, Chris slipped small amounts of salt into the sugar bowl as Gerrie looked and listened for someone coming. (It wasn't until the twins turned ten that they quit the sugar substitution. Almost immediately their mother once again learned how to make coffee that dad liked.)

On the way to their grandparents' house they sat in the back seat of the car and discussed whether they ought to change identities for two weeks. Since they had only seen grandma and grandpa twice before in their lives that they could remember, they decided against the switch. It would have been too easy and no challenge at all. Besides, each wanted to be remembered by her grandparents individually. The twin thing only went so far.

Having embraced both grandparents and informing them of particular identities, the twins received their room assignments.

"Chris and Gerrie, if it's okay, I've put both of you in the big bedroom at the top of the stairs with Kay. There are two double beds in that room and you girls can work out the arrangements."

The twins looked at each other and communicated in their own non-verbal, latent language. Gerrie told Chris it might be a good idea and it would be fun to have Kay in the room with them. Chris let Gerrie know that she agreed and besides, this was what grandma wanted.

"Sure, grandma," replied Chris, "we'll do it. It'll be a lot of fun. Let's go, Kay."

The two sets of parents wanted to go to the beach together and they left after a late lunch. After they departed grandpa announced that there would be no naps in the afternoons and no early bedtimes for the children during their stay. Of course this proclamation received shouts of approval. While it had been a long time since the girls had taken naps, Mick occasionally had to do so. He jumped in celebration and knew that he had a really neat grandpa.

Mick ran from the front of the house to the back saying, "Yes! Yes!"

Suddenly he stopped running and became silent. He stared out the wooden, cross-paned window at the back of the house. Without turning his head, Mick called out to the others.

"Hey, there's some real old guy in the backyard. Grampa, Grampa! Come here and look. There's a stranger sitting in your lawn chair."

The girls got there first and stared out the window. Gerrie said something to Chris that no one else heard. Chris replied out loud, "Probably, but I'm not sure."

Kay asked, "Grandpa, who is that? Do you know him?"

CHAPTER 2

A FRAIL, OLD MAN

In the backyard shade of a catalpa tree, a brittle, old man sat silently. His calloused hands and gnarled fingers rested on a walking stick. With the exception of several bare patches, a scraggly, gray beard covered his wrinkled, leathery face. His untrimmed mustache walrused down and over his hidden mouth. One of his weather-worn boots was untied. His dirty, faded socks no longer testified to their once white purity. A tattered, dark brown coat warmed him in the early afternoon of the August day. His baggy, black trousers produced several folds in his lap. Motionless, he rested on grandpa's homemade wooden chair. His glazed eyes remained fixed on an unseen object.

On the ground at the old man's side lay an aged dog. The two belonged together. Their facial expressions and energy levels appeared identical. Though it may seem difficult to imagine, the patriarchal animal appeared to be older than the dilapidated man.

Mick turned his eyes from the ancient pair and up to his grandpa. "Who is he, Grampa?"

Before he could answer, Gerrie asked, "Yes, grandpa, he is really old. Is he your dad?"

Grandma chuckled a second and grandpa replied, "No he's not my dad, but he is almost old enough to be. He's quite old and a very good friend of this family. His life has been a hard, difficult one with great suffering."

Kay asked, "I don't remember seeing him. Does he live here, grandpa?"

"Well, sort of. After his wife died, he hurt for a long time. For many years they had lived in a cabin high in the mountains. Since I retired and we moved, I had not seen him for almost five years. Then quite unexpectedly, last spring he came down from the north mountains and showed up here. We got up one morning and there he was sitting in that wooden chair."

Mick blurted out, "Has he stayed in the chair ever since he came here? He doesn't live in that chair does he?"

Grandpa gave a snorkeled laugh, "No, but it really might surprise you that he hasn't come into our house. He just won't do it."

Grandma added, "As much as we would like him to come inside, he won't. We take his meals out to him, but it really bothers me that he stays outside."

Ellen thought as she heard this and asked, "Where does he sleep?"

Grandpa replied, "He sleeps in the old hay loft over the storage barn. You kids have played in there. Remember?"

After the children voiced affirmation, grandpa continued. "In fact, he slept in there a couple of nights before we even knew he was here. He told me that if we didn't let him sleep in the hay loft, he would leave and not bother us again."

Grandma added once more, "Well, I can tell you that poor old man sleeping out there certainly does bother me."

"Me too," grandpa continued, "but there really is nothing that can be done. I have known him for some sixty years and he is one of the most determined men I have met. There is no reason to think that he is any different today."

Kay spoke with compassion, "Grandpa, you said he's had a hard, difficult life. Do you mean about his wife dying?"

"That's a part of it, and a real tough part at that. But, there was also his son. They had only one child, a boy. He died when just a youngster, probably around the age of one of you kids. They never had any more children. When his wife died after a painful illness, well, he was all alone. There are no other family members that I know of. I guess we're just about the closest thing to family he's got. He has hurt inside more than I care to imagine."

"That's really sad," said Gerrie, "I feel sorry for him."

Chris listened to her sister and then asked grandpa, "Do you think it might be okay to go out and talk to him?"

"Sure, but remember you have to speak loudly in his right ear. And, he is almost blind. He can only see a little bit out of one eye."

Gerrie asked, "How much can he see?"

"About a month ago I asked him about his eyesight and he let me know what it was like. He told me to think about being in a deep, dark well. You build a fire to keep warm. When the fire gets going, you cover it with a huge pile of wet pine needles. There are no flames and soon thick smoke filters up through the needles. The column of smoke ascends. Now, close one eye and look up. Above you is a hazy circle of light. That's what he told me it was like."

With a hint of fear, Kay said, "That's kind of scary. It makes me feel like I can't breathe because I am all closed in."

"That's the way he describes things. Maybe you children could get him to tell you a story."

"Grampa! What should we call him? He's not a grandpa like you, but that's not his fault. He's old enough to be a grandpa."

"Mick, why don't you and the others call him Great Grandpa? He might like that. Only one way to find out."

Gerrie sent a silent message to her twin. Chris pursed her lips in agreement and responded, "Isn't there some other name we could call him. What's his given name?"

Grandpa replied, "I tell you what. You young ones go ahead and introduce yourselves to him. He will let you know what you should call him. Since he can't see and has some difficulty with hearing, you'll have to touch him on the knee to let him know you are there and, I suppose, to wake him up."

The troop of five children stepped out the back door and slowly approached the old man. From the start, Mick found that he was in the front of the pack. They approached from the man's left side and noticed that his eyes were open and staring straight ahead. He blinked occasionally, but never noticed the children at his side. Though his eyes were open, he didn't appear to be aware of the children's presence. At the same time, the dog's eyes remained closed. Each of the children was certain that the dog knew they were there.

They stopped about ten feet from the old man. Kay leaned over and said something into Mick's ear. He responded with a loud whisper, "Why should I be the one who has to go up and touch his knee? Why don't you do it? That old dog might bite me."

Kay asked the rest of the group if they wanted to vote on the one to touch his knee. Mick knew what was coming and said that he'd do it.

Slowly he drew near the old man. Mick kept a close watch on the dog. Though the animal did not make even a twitching movement, the young boy knew that every move he made was being closely followed. No doubt, thought Mick, it was a mean and short-tempered old dog that had been in a lot of fights and had more than its share of wounds. Hoping to see the others waving him to return, the boy stopped and looked back. They silently motioned him to continue. Mick leaned forward, extended his pointer finger and lightly touched the old man's knee.

"Hello," replied the old man in a clear, matter-of-fact tone of voice.

"Hi," said Mick loudly, "did you hear me coming?"

"No, the dog let me know you and the others were here." Without moving his eyes, he raised his voice slightly, "You others, come closer." They did. "What's your name, boy?"

He answered and asked, "Mick. Can we call you Great-Grandpa?"

"How I wish you could, Mick, but you may not do so. I am not a great-grandpa."

"Can't we pretend?"

He replied, "You can, but you may not."

The man's reply made them a bit afraid. Kay questioned him, "I'm Kay. What should we call you?"

"You should call me what I am. Old Man. Just call me Old Man."

Ellen said, "I don't think we could do that, sir. Old Man is rather disrespectful."

He replied, "There is nothing disrespectful about either being old or being man. Old Man is a good name, for it is what I am. Which of you children will call me Old Man?"

No one said a word.

He continued, "Alright. Then which of you children has any objection to calling me Old One?"

Again, no one spoke.

He said, "Fine. Then Old One it is. When you speak to me, call me, Old One."

He stopped speaking. The children waited and looked at each other in silence.

Finally Mick asked, "What's the dog's name?"

The man did not reply.

He continued, only a bit louder, "Does the dog have a name?"

The man remained silent.

Ellen summoned some bravery and said, "Old One, my name is Ellen. Old One, what is the dog's name?"

"Hello Ellen. The dog has many names."

Mick understood now and asked, "Old One, what are some of the names of your dog?"

The old man spoke a bit sharply in reply, "Boy, you got it backwards."

While this was being said, Kay looked at the old dog. Mentally she noted its torn ear, a long scar over one eye and various healed-over scrapes, scratches, nicks and cuts from battles long since fought. But what she noticed the most was a long, wide pink scar from a wound that had sliced its dark nose. No doubt that wound was deep and took a long time to heal. However, Kay

17

could not see the wound that hurt the old dog the most. The dog had fought an enemy who crushed its right back paw. A foe had smashed all of the bones from its toe to the mid-point of its leg, including the pad of its heel. Of course, the children did not know this.

Chris thought of something and offered a query, "Old One, you said that the dog let you know that Mick and the rest of us were here. How did the dog let you know?"

"Of all people, you ought to know the answer to your question. Both of you know, don't you? Hah! You are surprised that others are also able to do it, aren't you?"

Kay turned to Chris and said, "What is he talking about, Chris?"

"Nothing."

Gerrie stepped in to direct the attention of the others, "Old One, will you tell us a story? I imagine that you know some great stories."

"You two make up quite a team. Identical twin sisters. You have diverted the conversation well. What is your name?"

"Gerrie. Old One, will you tell us a story?"

The old man laughed. "Very good, Gerrie. Do not fret. I will pursue that other business no further."

Kay became suspicious and whispered to Chris, "What is he talking about."

Chris replied, "Ask him if he'll tell us a story. I'll bet he knows some stories about royalty and high adventure in foreign kingdoms, like the rescue of a Czech princess. He might even have been a part of some great mystery."

Kay was sufficiently diverted. "Old One, please tell us a story."

"I know many stories. Some are short. Others are quite long. Most are true. The true ones often are filled with troubles. A few are fables. There are comedies and there are tragedies. They can be changed to avoid the pain and hurt. But a story it is, my young friends. So what shall it be?"

Ellen spoke first, "A long story, one very long."

"Do all of you have enough time for a long story?"

Ellen replied, "Yes. We have over thirteen days of vacation."

"I did not ask you how many days of vacation you had. I asked you if all of you had enough time. There is a great deal of difference, you know?"

Gerrie communicated a message to her sister. Chris smiled and spoke. "Old One, I think we have enough time if you have enough time."

A great laugh rumbled and erupted from deep within the old man. "Very good. You are probably quite right."

"Old One?"

"Yes, Mick."

"Tell us a long story that has a haunting echo that doesn't stop."

"A haunting echo that doesn't stop? Let me think a minute. ... Yes. Alright, let's begin."

CHAPTER 3

FIRST ECHO

The holy man spoke the ancient words as he held the baby in his strong arms. Of course, the baby did not know what the holy words meant.

The father tolerated the ceremony because it was expected of him and because he was afraid not to have this done. He was compelled to make this stop at the holy place. Making the more important visit to the body healer would also be required. That trip would be done this day as well. The baby's mother could not fathom the proceedings here. This was the first time she had ever been in a holy place. It all seemed a series of magical chants, incantations, actions and ritualistic applications. She allowed it as long as it remained words and ceremonies in which her son would not be in harm's way.

Oh children, little did she know the power of words and the adventures that accompany sacred acts.

The holy place, deserted except for the four people, dwarfed the quartet. The least number of candles had been lighted. The Candle of Holy Calling, the Candle of the Ear and the Candle of Sacred Stretching gave enough light for the ceremony, but did not enlighten the vaulted ceiling. The baby's back received support from the holy man's left forearm while the infant's head nestled in the palm of the overseer's hand. The small arms waved in random motions as his tiny, fully dilated, brown eyes peered without perception into the abyss of the cathedral ceiling.

Near the end of the ritual, the holy man slipped a white gown over the baby's head and covered both his small frame and the holy man's arm. The holy man bent his head forward and whispered into the little one's right ear. He did the same in the other ear. The holy man placed his right hand on the baby's chest long enough to speak some words. With three of his fingers he made a strange sign on the infant's forehead and breast. In the same position, he lifted the baby toward the ceiling. The holy man, with arms extended as far as possible, spoke the baby boy's name as loud as he was able.

"PICARO!"

The infant jerked instantly and his tiny arms reached out and up instinctively. The holy man repeated the name again. The baby, reacting as if mortally struck, inhaled an instant breath and closed his eyes. With split-second precision, the shout went forth from the guardian's lungs a third time. The baby's purple lips, pursed in a blood-filled curl, foretold an infant scream. The holy man remained still as he listened for the returning echoes from the high, elliptical ceiling.

"PICARO!" "PICARO!" "PICARO."

While the man's voice startled the boy's mother, the echoes made her shudder and draw her shawl closer over her shoulders. The holy man smiled, for he had heard the boy's name echo three times. This was good. For an instant, even the father was sobered by the sounds and overcome by the ceremony, as if he had heard the echoes before.

The holy man lowered the baby just as the infant's red face burst with quivering cries. He completed the ceremony with the ancient name and handed the baby to his mother. The familiar, comforting arms of his mother did not silence the boy. The sounds of the wailing infant displaced the echoed name and generated their own echoes. The three adults could not hear the boy's name echo a fourth time but it was much different for Picaro. The haunting echo never stopped for the rest of his life, though loud at certain times and on occasion, much softer. The sound heard in his soul never diminished. It only sharpened the longer he lived.

"Mr. Old One, that was a great story," replied Kay with all sincerity.

The old man spoke softly, "Hush now, Kay. This is only the introduction. It is a good beginning, but we are only at the start."

"Wow," said Mick, "he's only at the beginning. This is gonna be great!"

Kay smiled.

Ellen twirled her hair and waited.

Chris and Gerrie spoke in their own way.

"Should I go on with it?"

All five children responded in unison, "Yes!"

"Please," added Mick, "it's a great story."

The old man said, "Good. This is a pretty good story. I wonder how it's going to end. Now, where was I? Oh yes."

Picaro's father, a strong man named Mac, quickly returned to his natural frame of mind. Swiftly, he ushered his wife and son out of the holy place, muttering something about a worthless, superstitious old fool who couldn't make a living with honest work.

Eliza held her son tightly and scurried, partly because the holy place unnerved her and mostly because Mac pushed his wife in the middle of her back. She asked what was wrong and he snapped back, "Be quiet and keep walking. That's done. I don't want to set foot in that place again."

"What if we have another child?"

"Look, woman. I told you to be quiet. We have to go to the body healer. At least she will do us some good. I'll have to pay her something, but it will be worth it for my son. Then we go home. I have another appointment and then I must go to work at the mill."

Eliza knew what appointment her husband wanted to keep. One of the dens of strong drink would take some of their money in the afternoon.

Several hundred feet outside the entrance to the holy place, a red-bearded man in a plaid coat saw them. The young man had been sitting along the side of the path. As they approached, he stood and put himself in their way and motioned them to stop. He said nothing to either of them, but handed a card to Mac.

```
    I am Walter the Acolyte from the
       ancient village of Benedicamus
         at the base of High Mountain.
            I may not speak to you.
       (Please return this card to me
           after you have read it.)
```

Eliza asked her husband, "What is it?"

"Nothing. A bunch of nonsense."

He handed the card back to the young man and attempted to move on. Walter the Acolyte remained in place as Mac started to walk. They bumped together and Mac was jostled by the young man. In one sweeping motion, Mac raised his forearm and struck the red-bearded man on the side of the face. Walter the Acolyte lay on the side of the path stunned and silent.

"Stay out of my way, fool. Let's go, Eliza. You want me to carry Picaro?"

"No, he's fine."

Within the hour the couple arrived at the shack of the body healer. In those days a body healer not only helped someone who was sick or injured, but also gave them potions to keep them from getting various diseases. This was particularly important for babies since forest fever was deadly. The healer in Woods Town was a recluse known as Edith the Quiet. While she was a strange woman who kept to herself, she was kind and gentle. She had immense compassion for the children, especially the babies.

After Eliza introduced Picaro to Edith the Quiet, the body healer went inside her old shack for the needed potions and returned momentarily.

In a screechy voice, Edith the Quiet informed the couple, "Recently I took a long walk in the small woods to the far west. A young plant has shared its great gift with me. Three drops of this on Picaro's tongue and he will be safe from forest fever."

Picaro worked his little mouth in a sucking motion as the woman placed the drops onto his tongue. An instant later he gave a grimace and shuddered from its taste. The body healer looked into his ears. Everything was fine. She opened his eyes and placed a drop of high spring water into each of them. Edith the Quiet smiled and assured Eliza that she had a healthy baby.

While the two women spoke, Mac reached into his coat pocket for some money to give to the body healer. His hand discovered something in addition to his money, another card from Walter the Acolyte.

> *The Hunter is after you.*
> *The Wind has given your scent*
> *to His Hound.*
> *At this very moment*
> *His Hound is tracking you.*

A momentary chill penetrated Mac's shoulders and a shiver waved along his back. He had the fearful feeling that someone or something lurked behind him. Mac attempted to nullify its effects and shrug it off. Often it gnawed at his soul in the stillness of a sleepless night. Today he listened intently for the baying of a hound. He heard nothing.

"Fool," he muttered, "he must have slipped this in my pocket when he bumped me. It's a wonder he didn't take my money."

He nearly threw the card away when he noticed something written on the other side.

> *"Holy Writ must be taken away,"*
> *Or so, the skeptics do say,*
> *"There's no benediction,*
> *it's all myth and just fiction."*
> *And they tell us to "have a nice day!"*

In disgust, Mac threw the card to the ground and stepped on it with the heel of his logging boot using a twisting motion to grind it into the dirt. He mumbled something about people not having much to do but sit around handing out stupid little cards.

After paying the standard fee to Edith the Quiet, he led his wife and son away from her shack. His thirst heightened and he wanted to arrive at his appointment early that afternoon. The trip to Upper Woods Camp would take more than three hours because there was only a trail leading to it. He hurried the woman along ...

"Excuse me, Mr. Old One," interrupted Ellen, "but what is a *benediction*? It sounds like a strange word."

"No, it's not a strange word. It's really a good word," answered the frail old man.

"I'm sure it is, sir," said Ellen, "but what does it mean?"

He replied, "I just told you."

CHAPTER 4

INFANT NIGHTMARE

After the old man fell asleep in the warmth of the August afternoon, the children went into the house for grandma's homemade lemonade. Chris drank hers quickly. She was the searcher, looking intently and doing what it took to find something or someone. That afternoon she wanted to look in grandma's dictionary for a few words she did not understand from the story. (This is usually a wise thing for anyone to do.)

The children agreed that someone should always be watching the old man. When he woke, they wanted to go back to him so he would continue the story. An hour later Kay announced that he was awake. They hurried to him and three of them touched his knee.

"Hello," said the old man.

Ellen replied, "Good afternoon, Old One."

The expression on his face changed for a moment as he responded, "Old one? Oh, yes, Old One. It's you children, isn't it?"

"Yes, Old One, it's us," said Mick, "we want you to continue your story. Will you?"

"Well, yes, I suppose so," he answered. "But what story was it, and where were we in my story?"

Gerrie was quick to reply, "You were telling us about Mac and Eliza taking baby Picaro to Upper Woods."

"Oh yes, now I remember."

Before he could begin once again, Gerrie asked, "Old One, is this story real?"

The old man grinned and said, "The place is in a land not here. The time is from an age not now. The customs and rituals are of a people who never were. So yes, little one, the story is quite real."

Gerrie was puzzled. "Old One, that doesn't make any sense to me."

"I know, Gerrie. You will have to grow much younger before it all begins to mean something."

"This is getting boring," said Mick. "Old One, may we get back to the story?"

The expression on the old man's face was 70% grin and 70% grimace. "Get back? We never left it. You must remember that the hunt continues to the end. The hunt is older than all creation."

Mick sighed and said, "What was Upper Woods Camp like?"

The old man smiled and continued his story.

Northland was a large, unmapped part of the land in those days. Woods Town was one of Northland's many small communities serving as supply centers for the people. Upper Woods Camp, up river from Woods Town, emerged from the wilderness and began as a remote logging camp with a large sawmill beside the creek.

There were only two ways to Upper Woods Camp, the first by water and no one went that way since Bad Spirit River allowed sturdy boats and canoes to float down. But it flowed with such swiftness that no one attempted to make an upstream return. That left the long hike up the path along the north side of the river. One creek forked off and had to be crossed by a footbridge made from a fallen old growth fir tree. The footing on this six-foot diameter log always seemed dangerous. Snow, rain and even the morning dew made it slippery. The next stream, Falls Creek, forked off from Bad Spirit River to the northeast. An hour's hike along Falls Creek brought the traveler to the small waterfall and Upper Woods Camp.

The camp consisted of twenty shacks on one side of the creek for living, the mill on the other for working and one den of strong drink for keeping appointments. The only plumbing for each shack was a cold water tap for the sink. Randomly located outhouses served the entire camp. The interiors of the identical shacks were constructed with a small kitchen in one corner and a wood stove in the opposite corner. This permitted beds in the remaining corners, two in the far corner and one by the door. No walls divided the space within the shacks.

The energy from the waterfall had been tapped and now powered the mill. Years earlier the men formed a quarter-acre log pond by diverting the creek into a dugout area. A large landing on the uphill side of the pond received the logs. The buckers worked on the landing before rolling the logs into the pond.

Chris waited for him to hesitate in the story and said, "Old One, tell us about Picaro and his parents."

The story-teller replied, "Ahh, too much setting up of the scene, huh? Okay."

Mac divided his time between the mill as a foreman, the den as a drinker and the shack as a sleeper. The drinking had not become serious until the last year when, as foreman, Mac hired an older boy to work as a boom-man. The boom-man, named Karl, worked alone on the logs in the pond. He used a long pole with an end that had a point and a hook on it. Karl jumped from log to log as he pushed and pulled logs into position to be caught by the bull chain. One day, the young man slipped as he jumped from one log to another. Karl hit his head on one of the logs, knocked himself out, fell into the pond and drowned.

The young man's death devastated Mac. He knew the Hunter had taken the young man but this was too soon because Karl had so much of his life still to live. Mac tried to purge the incident from his mind by immersing himself in the spirits of the den. The strong drink numbed his thoughts and prevented him from hearing the howl of the hunting hound. But strong drink stops neither the Hunter nor his hound.

Picaro's first home was there in Upper Woods. Even though it became a painful life for Mac and a lonely one for Eliza, Picaro was loved. His small bed, pushed into the right front corner of the shack, provided protection from the cold nights. It was in that bed, shortly after his calling in the holy place, that Picaro had his first nightmare.

"Tell us about his nightmare!"

"Yes, please do," chimed in the others.

"But children," said the old man, "I'm not sure that I should tell you about nightmares, especially this nightmare."

"Please."

"Well I could, but remember, a baby's nightmare is not filled with detail. There are general pictures that trouble and basic longings just out of reach. This is true of Picaro's first bad dream."

The children waited in silent anticipation.

Picaro sat alone on something like a strange shore with no sand, no trees, no rocks, no people and no sounds. An island was a short distance, perhaps only two feet from the shore. The baby could see the entire island. It remained barren except for the dark shadow of a tall, leafless, crooked tree. A yellow sea of thick goo with large lumps surrounded the island. The baby could not see through the yellow goo. The large lumps made the surface uneven and horrible black objects of sharpness stuck out from many of the lumps of the yellow goo.

Picaro longed to get to the island. He had to get there. He was legally required, compelled, drawn, pushed and forced. The island was almost within reach, two short feet, a mere twenty-four

inches. No matter, he could not get there. He remained compelled; he had to get to that island. He was too weak. Sleep would make him stronger and he would be able to get there when stronger.

Such a great yearning. Such a short distance, about the length of his own body. He fell asleep on the shore.

After his sleep, he felt stronger, more agile, more capable. Picaro looked to the island and unnamed terror invaded his infant body. The island was farther away. Panic overwhelmed him. Need and despair consumed him. Fright shook his body. Quivering, the baby arms reached up and into the darkness of the night. The cry of terror violently burst from infant lungs and pierced the midnight air. A couple seconds later, the familiar voice and the consoling arms of his mother tried to comfort him.

Throughout his childhood, Picaro's mind conjured the same dream. Each time the images became clearer and his thoughts more expressible. The yellow goo was not solid enough for walking nor liquid enough for swimming. The large lumps of jagged clumps of cutting clutter remained ready to slice the boy. These dark, crystallized metal shards erupted from the yellow goo. Beneath the surface were hidden snares even deadlier.

Still, getting to the island was not optional. It had to be done. A basic drive and an instinctive need to get to the island caused the boy to experience an anxiety that permeated him - body and soul and spirit. The boy remained never quite able to begin the journey across the yellow goo. The dream compelled him to get there, but he never got beyond a sense of the inability to begin. That forced feeling evolved into a nightmare. He needed more strength and that meant more sleep on the beach. However, each time he arose from sleeping on the beach, the island was farther away. He needed time to get the strength he required. During that time the island moved farther from him. The insurmountable gulf between him and the island in his first nightmare became more impossible, indeed, a greater infinity each time the dream returned. A great, growing, impassable gulf separated him from the island. Now the island appeared as a dark spot on the horizon.

Despair turned to an utter, hopeless, frantic, frozen anxiety. Picaro could not move one inch in the direction of the island and it was at this point in his bad dream, he always woke trembling and in tears. After each nightmarish episode, Picaro realized that the older he became, the farther away he remained. The best and closest opportunity for him to make it to the island was as a weak, helpless infant. Though impossible then, it would have been easier than now. This horrible nightmare continued until Picaro became an older teenager.

Chris said, "Old One, what made the nightmare stop?"

The old man replied, "Well, the last time he had the dream, the island was a black dot on the sea of yellow goo. The dot looked no different than the dark metal shards. Picaro could no longer see the island. That was the last time."

Ellen had been listening intently. Finally she asked, "Old One, what was it that made baby Picaro have the yearning to get to the island?"

The old man replied, "Not *what*, Ellen. No, not *what* at all. Rather, your question should be *who*? -- *who* put that desire into the infant?"

Mick rose up, "Well, who was it that would do such a wicked thing?"

"No, not who *was* it? But who *is* he?"

Mick continued, "Who is he?"

"Yes," chimed the others, "who is he?"

The old man leaned forward on his walking stick. Staring through them with blind eyes, he whispered to the children, "The Hunter."

CHAPTER 5

THE OTHER

After supper and chores, the five children asked the old man to continue the story. He agreed, but said he would have to stop if the evening turned too cool. He did not want to get a chill in his shoulders and back. This was fine with the cousins. They wanted to hear more of the story. With his eyes open and his hands on the walking stick, the old man continued.

Some of Picaro's first memories included standing and walking and standing and waiting. At the end of most days, Eliza took Picaro to the den of strong drink. There the two of them stood waiting outside while Mac sat inside taking care of his appointed rounds and wagering with the other men. At times he tricked them out of drinks. Once he got four drinks when he demonstrated how he could jump higher than the tallest fir in the woods. Sometimes he won glasses of strong drink by betting. For example, the others claimed Mac could never father a son. He bet heavily on this one and after the birth of Picaro, Mac drank for a week without having to pay any money.

His wife and son stood outside. Though the men within teased him about the woman checking on him, they did not take the teasing too far. Mac was a tough, experienced fighter and he usually came out on top in a fight. Sometimes he stepped outside to yell at Eliza. At other times he did so to settle a dispute. He called her names and told her to go home. She stayed. Late in the evening he staggered from the den, picked up Picaro and walked to the shack.

In the years that followed, Picaro had two younger brothers, Anton and Dave. After they were born, Eliza no longer stood and waited outside the den. One morning she took her three sons and left Mac. She moved farther into the forests of Northland to an area with two sawmills. To those who knew this place, it was called The Dell. A small creek ran between the two mills. Stands of cottonwood, alder and ash grew along the water. The men felled fir trees from the nearby hills and mountains.

The tar-papered shack, not used by anyone, sheltered them from the rain and cold. Eliza placed the beds in the same position as she had in the shack at Upper Woods. Picaro's bed was next to the front door which would remain closed and secure only if Eliza wedged a table knife into the jamb.

Picaro began working in the woods and in the mills at the age of five. He had the little jobs, the ones he could both learn and do, like setting the small choker. He enjoyed this job because he could stand on the log as the cable dragged it to the mill landing. He piled the slab wood and took care of the edgings. Picaro crawled under the deck and shoveled out the piles of sawdust under the edger and headsaw. He handed strips to the men who stacked the lumber in rows to air-dry. He hauled gunnysacks of fir sawdust for the big stove and emptied them into the sheet metal hopper. There had to be enough sawdust in the hopper to burn all night.

Shortly after moving into The Dell, young Picaro became aware of the Other. That awareness was stronger at night, though it also did descend upon him at various places during the day. The crawl space under the shack was one place he never went. The darkness of the hole combined with the closed-in space kept him away. The Other might stay there during the day as a place to wait for the night, or to wait for some silly boy to come crawling into its lair. Shadowy closets, a long hallway and dark rooms, especially like those in CJ's house scared Picaro.

Another place able to frighten the young boy during the day was the outhouse. There was no toilet in the shack. Eliza and her sons used an outhouse about thirty feet behind the shack. The roof had been constructed incorrectly and thus allowed the rain to run off the eaves in front of the outhouse entryway. The door of the faded red outhouse remained permanently open. No matter, for even if he could, Picaro would never have closed the door because the small room would have been without light. Even with the door open in the daylight, the hole below was filled with shadows. The opening on the bench led to the dark pit below and that smelly abyss was just the sort of place where the Other stayed. So more often than not, Picaro found relief elsewhere.

The deep parts of the woods behind his house were also places the Other might be. At the edge of the woods, Picaro, Anton and Dave would play, explore and build forts. Sides were taken as they tried to hit each other with fir cones. These battles usually ended when one of them was hit in the face with a green fir cone. They climbed up, bounced on and swung down the larger vine maples. Thick, low fir boughs posed as bucking broncos to be tamed. Crawling under the canopy of tall ferns and making dams in the small creek occupied hours and days of the three boys.

At times Picaro was particularly mean to his brothers. He might lure them back to the limits of the deeper woods and suddenly yell, "Bear! Monster! Run, It's gonna get you!" Picaro sprinted to the house and left his slower brothers scrambling behind him. Dave cried and ran, ran and cried as he toddled at a slow pace, occasionally tripping over a small, fir limb or a downed fern stem. But even at such times, Picaro never crossed the line into the deeper woods. They never violated the unspoken rule: Do not go so far into the woods that you are not able to see the shack. The three boys avoided the Other's domain in the deeper woods.

Of course, if an adult like their mother or Bud walked with them, they could go back there and be safe. The Other had to give way to grownups. You see, Picaro actually believed the Other was afraid of adults. He thought the Other only wanted children.

Mick interrupted with a question, "Old One, was the Other the same as the Hunter?"

The old man replied, "Now you children must remember this from Picaro's point of view. He didn't know of the Hunter by that name, or for that matter, that the Hunter existed."

"Who did he think the Other was?"

"If you asked him to tell you who the Other was, without using the word 'other,' he would have said a monster, the monster, fear, dread or *It*."

Mick replied, "I agree! Those might be good names for the Hunter."

Chris changed the direction of the conversation, "What about Picaro and the Other at night? You said he was most aware of the Other when it was dark."

"I am not sure I should tell you about all of this," said the old man in a changed tone.

Mick asked, "Why not, Old One?"

"I know why," replied Ellen. "He thinks he'll scare us."

The old man agreed, "Yes, Ellen. You've been frightened before, especially at night. Perhaps I should pass by this part of Picaro's life."

Ellen continued, "Please, Old One. This situation is quite different and it won't bother me."

Interested in her comment, the old man prompted Ellen, "Different? How?"

"Well, I am never frightened of monsters, spirits or demons. It is always bad people who are after me. I hear in the news that someone has committed a crime and my imagination runs away. I think the criminal is under my bed. So when I have to go to bed, I look under it from a distance. Then I run and jump into my bed, hoping he won't reach out a hand and grab me before I make it. When I was younger, I thought if I went to sleep before my parents did, I would be safe. I tried but I always heard my dad snoring first. Then I stayed awake most of the night. Quite silly, huh?"

An immediate response came from the story-teller, "No, Ellen! Not silly at all. If Picaro heard you, he would understand you completely. Should I continue then?"

"Yes," came the quick reply from the children.

Picaro did not fear that some wicked human being lurked about or was sneaking around to get him, either slipping under his bed or hiding in the shack. Rather, the young boy had a fear of the

Other. Though he believed no human being to be outside the high window above his bed, he was also convinced that if he stood on his bed and looked out the window at night, the Other, in human form, would be pressed against the glass.

The Other came in several ways. First, there were the dark places of the night where the Other hid, especially the full moon nights when the Other cloaked itself in the shadows cast by buildings and trees. When there was cloud-cover and the wind blew, the Other moved freely. *It* swam from tree to tree making the same swishing sound as the wind does when blowing through needles of the evergreens.

The young boy also knew that the Other entered by way of dreams which *It* turned into nightmares. For weeks after a bad dream, Picaro remained afraid to go to sleep. He tried to stay awake by creating good stories and exciting adventures in his mind. Sometimes he thought about his father and wondered if he would ever see him again. But the mind can only maintain such thoughts and stories for awhile and then, sometime during the darkness of the night, the boy would fall asleep. For his sake, he was unaware of the drowsiness that finally and mercifully overwhelmed him.

The Other also appeared in the form of a monster, demon or animal. On one still, quiet night, Picaro heard a chilling shriek outside the shack. It sounded like a woman screaming. The next day he asked his mother if she had heard it. Eliza said she had and thought it might have been a cougar because sometimes their snarling in the night seemed like a woman's screaming. Picaro had the Other thoughts about *It*.

On one clear night the boy heard something outside the door of the shack. At first he thought he imagined it. However, upon closer listening, he heard sniffing sounds at the bottom of the door and the padded noises of an animal walking back and forth on the wooden porch. Picaro looked at the table knife wedged between the door and its jamb. The handle of the knife reflected a moon beam. The handle of the door did not latch but served only for gripping to push the door open or to pull it shut. A faded piece of cloth covered nine small window panes in the upper half of the door. Long springs at the top and bottom held the curtain securely in place. One of the window panes had been broken and a flimsy piece of cardboard covered the hole.

On that night Picaro did something that was very much unlike him. The sniffing at the bottom of the door and the pacing continued. As quietly as possible, he scooted to the head of his bed, pulled up his legs, got on his knees and leaned over to look out the lower left window pane. He moved the curtain to the side, far enough to look out with one eye. The pacing stopped.

Outside his door a large animal listened. Picaro could not see the animal's head as the beast silently sniffed at the door sill. Picaro could see the animal from the shoulders back to the tail and determined it to be larger than a fox. Coyotes roamed the area, but this animal didn't have the coyote's tail. It might have been a wolf, but the fur seemed too short. There were wild dogs in The Dell, but they usually ran in packs.

While Picaro made his one-eyed observations, the animal sensed the boy's awareness. Picaro released the curtain, backed from the door and pulled the covers over his head. There in the darkness of his small, undercover world, the boy confirmed what he already knew; the Other had been after him, and now, the Other knew where Picaro lived.

"I think we better stop right there," said the old man.

Mick, frustrated at having to stop at this point in the story, spoke without thinking, "Why, Old One? Because it's getting dark outside?"

The old man asked, "Is it getting dark outside now? With my dim eyes I didn't know."

Everyone felt sad about this, especially Mick. He realized he had made a mistake.

Kay the compassionate rescued her brother from his predicament by asking the old man, "Are you getting a chill, Old One?"

"Yes. You must get inside. Me too. Good night."

The cousins said good night to him and went into the house, and for one reason or another, none of them slept right away.

CHAPTER 6

ON THE RUN

The children hardly spoke the next morning, each one reflecting on the previous day's episode and anticipating the continuing story. After breakfast one of them reported that the frail man was not sitting in the chair yet. This gave them plenty of time to finish their chores. As they went back and forth with their work, each of the children checked to see if the old man had appeared. At midmorning he came out of the storage barn and hobbled to the chair. The dog limped along keeping beside the mysterious old man and waited until the man was seated before assuming its post next to him.

Gerrie noticed the old pair first and quickly passed the word to the others. They abandoned the busy work, their chores long since completed in anticipation of the old man and his haunting story. Several long pieces of straw clung to the old man's clothing. Kay greeted him for the group. He said good morning and immediately resumed the story.

Picaro grew strong and lean with the work in the woods and at the mills. At fourteen, he did the work of a man. He helped the fallers carry the saws. He checked the cuts and wedged the trees. He wielded a double-bit axe for limbing the fallen trees. This became especially dangerous in the spring of the year when the sap was up on the alder trees.

Picaro enjoyed a particular feeling of satisfaction to work the entire morning falling the tall trees in a small part of the vast woods for he knew that the afternoon light would pour into the newly exposed area. A section of the wild woods had been opened up for people. However, this was not the main reason Picaro experienced such satisfaction. Oh no, dear children, for the young man named Picaro, this clear-cutting signified a small victory, a setback for the Other. A tiny part of the dominion of *It* had been lost. An acre of cover, shadowy places and dark holes no longer existed for the Other.

Most of Picaro's work took place in The Dell's mills, usually off-bearing in both Bud's alder mill with the short logs and in Pappy's fir mill. The fir logs were twelve to sixteen feet long while special orders for timbers up to thirty feet long could be filled. In Picaro's hands, the long-handled, pointed peavey became a useful, powerful tool at the mill landing. He used the short, snub-nosed peavey with skill and precision inside the mill near the headrig and at the carriage.

While much of the work remained dull and boring, Picaro did learn to endure and work. The continuous noise in the sawmills left long periods of time for thinking. The constant droning of the saws, the familiar sounds of the carriage as it traveled from one end to the other and the singing of the ball-bearing rollers did not permit conversation.

The community established a school in Upper Woods and required Picaro's attendance. Schooling seemed fine but the young man was not particularly interested. He had no need for it, especially if he remained working in the woods and at the mills. He routinely returned home from school in the late afternoon and, after eating supper, began off-bearing. He worked in Bud's sawmill for three to four hours before stopping for the night.

Along with Eliza and his two brothers, Picaro lived a quarter mile up the road from the mill. It was always dark when Picaro finished working at the sawmill. Since no one else lived between his home and the sawmill, Picaro traveled alone during his trip home. This meant he had to travel by himself during the darkness of and through the awful places inhabited by the Other.

Picaro raced the entire way to the shack. When he got within sight of the shack, he stopped to recuperate from the gauntlet just run. He did not want to enter the shack breathing heavily and with heart pounding. He would not let Eliza or his younger brothers see him frightened. Picaro thought it unmanly to be afraid, to cry or to call out for help. He believed that sort of thing was reserved for babies and young children. He made that run a thousand times and each time it was a frightening experience for him. But, do you know when he was the most terrified during the run?

"No," said two of the children.
"When it was the darkest," suggested Chris.
"When it was the quietest?" asked Mick.

You might think that he would be the most afraid when the dense cloud cover made it the blackest or when silence reigned over the land. But at those times he saw nothing and heard nothing. He charged into the still darkness and ran until he drew near the shack. Indeed, what frightened him the most was the gauntlet home on the clear nights when a light breeze blew across the land. This was especially the case when snow blanketed Alf's field to the left and the flowing darkness of the awful woods to the right fell across his path and the wind gently rustled the underbrush. On such wicked nights the sharpened shapes and the shifting shades and the shimmering shadows conjured images to his eyes, communicated evil to his ears and suggested all manner of dreaded horror to his mind. A dark clump of short bushes against the white snow might be two wolves stalking him. A shadowy, vine maple silhouetted against the white and rattling in the wind could be the Other welling up from the depths of an earthly grave.

A young man's imagination runs wild at such times and Picaro's was no exception. Just when he convinced himself of the foolishness of what he thought he saw and believed he heard on his nightly run and just when he would start to attribute it to a childhood fantasy and a creative imagination, the startling reality confronted him.

He encountered the first reality on one of those awful nights, a time when it was not especially clear, one not too dark, one not too breezy though certainly not quiet. Picaro began his run as usual. The shadows of the trees draped across the trail and swayed in the breeze as if to gather any sojourner into itself with the dark, sweeping limbs. While in full sprint, Picaro raced into a large shadowy area and nearly ran into a deer. The animal jumped to the left and loped across the field. At the same instant another deer, standing in waist high brush to his right, began running. The crinkly leaves of the salal bushes magnified the sound of the beast's escape a hundred times. For months after this encounter, Picaro did not run as fast and kept his eyes fixed on the path.

Another time, on a clear, cold night with a whisper of wind, he made his dash for the shack. The frigid air penetrated to the depths of his lungs and made his eyes water as he ran. From over his right shoulder a silent, black shadow glided by him, no more than five feet from him as it passed over. He covered his mouth with his hand to keep from beckoning the shadow with a scream of terror. The Other came to mind instantly. Whoever or whatever or whichever, it skimmed above the surface of the snow-white field for several seconds. Suddenly it enlarged, dropped to the ground and vanished. Picaro never stopped running. He kept his watery eyes on it and on the place where it disappeared. Later, he convinced himself it was an owl gliding to a stealthy kill. Or, as he pondered all these things, he believed it may have been an owl on patrol in the service of the Other. Or, he thought it might be one of the many manifestations of the Other.

That night, as he lay in bed, he resolved to leave The Dell as soon as he completed his schooling. Besides, he questioned the authority of his mother more often and frequently challenged her. The frustration of working with no future except working more and living in the awful place increased. Picaro saw young men work until they became older and it seemed to him that when they got old enough, most made standing appointments at the dens of strong spirits. The young Picaro, now bursting into adulthood, hated those dens as much as he hated his father. He loathed Mac. He despised the man who caused so much hurt and heartache for Eliza, for his brothers and for him. Under no circumstances would Picaro permit himself to follow in his father's staggering footsteps. He wanted to leave this all behind, along with the Other who had plagued him ever since he came to The Dell. Setting out on one's own and starting all over with a new life sounded so appealing.

The next week at school, Picaro heard of a war being waged in a distant land. He began his preparations to depart and become a warrior.

CHAPTER 7

PURSUED

The story-teller lowered his head as if either tired from the tale or meditating on an important point. The children waited, wondering if the old, frail-looking man needed to rest. After they reluctantly suggested that he take a break, they silently rejoiced when he continued with the story.

Two days after finishing school the following spring, Picaro left. He kissed his mother the traditional good-by and ceremoniously touched his brothers while uttering the familiar departure, "Gotcha last!" Off he ran before Anton and Dave could react and try to touch him last.

He stowed everything in a burlap bag hoisted high on his back and held in place with a belt and a length of rope. As he left The Dell behind he felt the freedom he had anticipated. His spirit soared as he was finally on his own. He stopped long enough in Upper Woods Camp to visit a couple of friends and especially to say farewell and execute the "gotcha last" to his best friend, Araunah. Several of his school friends made plans to leave within the week. Two others he visited said they would leave before fall. Araunah decided to stay. All vowed to return in two years and share war stories. Little did they know that not all would return, and of those still alive who did, not one of them would ever be able to come home. Oh, many returned to Upper Woods Camp to meet years later, but neither it nor they were ever the same again.

  Picaro left Upper Woods Camp to make the journey to Woods Town. He followed Falls Creek to its end, where the creek emptied into Bad Spirit River. The clear air heightened his mental sharpness and the spring weather reflected Picaro's mood: bright and promising. Old Growth Bridge, built some seven years earlier, replaced the ancient tree from which the old footbridge was made and named. Walking across the bridge caused the young man to reflect. He had never been this far alone. The few times he had traveled to Woods Town were with his mother or with a mill boss. The trips to Woods Town had only been to particular places and could hardly be called visits. Except for the metal works shop at the north edge and a dry goods store near it, Woods Town remained unknown to and unexplored by Picaro.

  In a short time he arrived at the northern edge of town. His pace slowed as he eyed buildings and people. He moved to the western side of the main road where he could be out of the way as he gazed through shop windows. People seemed neither friendly nor hostile, just busy. No one paid particular attention to him, or for that matter, to one another. They ignored each other as they passed on the side of the street just as they ignored Picaro. Though he understood this for himself since he was the stranger in town, he could not comprehend their disregard for one another.

  When convinced that no one in the town had a friendly demeanor, an older man smiled at him, slapped him on the back and asked him if he was out on his own. Picaro grinned and opened his mouth to respond. He stopped short in his reply when he realized that the older man had made the comment in passing, in a manner obviously desiring no answer.

After slowly walking up and down the main part of town, and taking the better part of an hour to do so, Picaro realized his hunger. A side road to the east looked as if it would lead to a quiet place where he could eat. A tree several hundred feet away looked inviting. On the way, he noticed a middle-aged man sitting to the side of a grassy lane. When he saw Picaro coming, the blond-headed man stood up, approached the young man and gave him a card. Picaro watched the blond-headed man and waited. The man motioned his head to the card, obviously desiring that Picaro read it. Without taking his eyes from the blond-headed man, Picaro raised the card. The man nodded again and Picaro read.

> I am Jerome the Kantor from the
> ancient village of Benedicamus
> at the base of High Mountain.
> I may not speak to you.
> (Please return this card to me
> after you have read it.)

The puzzled young man looked at him and read the card a second time. Picaro returned the card to Jerome the Kantor and smiled. Jerome the Kantor returned the smile. The young man remained silent. (Picaro, you see, made the common mistake of thinking that because someone could not speak, he was also not able to hear. If the truth be known, Jerome the Kantor possessed excellent hearing as well as fine speech capabilities. Rather, Jerome the Kantor lacked permission.)

Without warning, the blond-headed man slapped Picaro on the back and walked away. This seemed bizarre to the young man. He attempted to understand what the encounter with the blond-headed man might mean. While the card puzzled the young man, the blond-headed man's behavior seemed stranger. Picaro concluded that the back-slapping was this people's equivalent of his farewell custom of "gotcha last." As he walked, he put Jerome the Kantor out of his thoughts.

Picaro saw a tree ahead and decided to eat his lunch under it. He approached the targeted tree and noticed an impressive structure a short distance along the lane. As a boy, Picaro grew up surrounded by large mills and dry kilns. The structure down the path seemed unusually tall and this attracted Picaro's attention. The location of the building, tucked into the woods with the roof rising above the canopy of the woods, intrigued him. He could not imagine what purpose it served. He determined to investigate the high, domed building after he had eaten.

Picaro sat under a large cedar tree the limbs of which had been trimmed to ten feet. A cool spring breeze whispered through its green branches. Picaro took a small loaf of bread and two chunks of cheese from the food can in his pack. Halfway through his lunch, he discovered a card in his pocket. He looked back in the direction of Jerome the Kantor. The lane back to the center of town was deserted. Picaro popped the last piece of cheese in his mouth and read the card.

```
The Hunter is after you.
The Wind has given your scent
        to His Hound.
    At this very moment
His Hound is tracking you.
```

Immediately, three reactions dominoed and overwhelmed Picaro. Fear came first. The Other was supposed to be confined to a certain geographical area and *It* had been left behind at home. The young man assumed that he left his anxiety and uneasy spirit at Falls Creek as well. The idea suddenly occurred to him that a different Dread haunted each region. This possibility had never occurred to him and until the instant he comprehended the message on the card, the thought that some other Other stalked the people in the area of Woods Town had never surfaced in his mind. He had no idea then. He did now. The card, with its immediate threat of Picaro's being known and pursued, instantly awakened yesterday's fear.

Such servile fear ushered in varying angers. Reactionary anger rose from within and focused on the Idea. Picaro directed seething anger at the Idea. He rediscovered or conjured, he could not say which nor deny the possibility of both, that the Idea remained the overall, unwritten, underlying law. These forces plagued innocent children's dreams, infiltrated the nightmares of the youth and terrorized the mind of man. This Idea permitted territorial forces to haunt people's lives in many and various ways.

A formed, resentful anger replaced the spontaneous anger and Picaro directed it at the Hunter. The Other, less defined and apparently less powerful than the Hunter, had been a manageable *It*. Picaro confined the Other to shadows, dark places and dreams. Besides, no one ever spoke to Picaro about the Other and he had never mentioned *It* to anyone in his eighteen years of life. The Idea, deeper than the Other and origin of every *It*, had now become manifest in the Hunter. This *It* revealed himself as well as the sport of its game. This *It* had become so well known that people under the Hunter's influence distributed cards with announcements that warned and threatened. The Hunter pursued people and had a hound to do the dirty work in tracking down the hapless prey. The Other only waited for a child to walk into its darkened lair. Except for nightmares, the Other could be avoided. The Hunter was different and arrogant enough to be revealed and identified. The Hunter was a pursuing *It*. This greater *It* and the hound would not permit their prey any rest. There was no peace with this *It*. Picaro concluded that the Hunter must be resisted and hated at all times and with all energies of body, resources of mind, determination of will and strength of soul directed to the task. Staying away from the Hunter and one step ahead of the hound would not be easy. Picaro determined to leave this land of the

Hunter and to get far away from this region where the hound engaged in such mischievous, sadistic sport.

Alas! How Picaro hated the Hunter! An anger, wrought from frustration and fueled by disappointment, heightened his hatred and resolve. Only this morning Picaro experienced freedom and now he was compelled to run each day, moving from this land to the next and always looking over his shoulder.

These temporal angers gave way to anxiety and doubt. Before he entered this town, he had been an unknown to the Hunter. Not so any longer. Something within caused Picaro to feel that once known, one was always known to the Hunter. Could the young man ever be able to get far enough away so that the wind did not give scent to the hound? So that the Hunter would forget him? How far would the Hunter and that hound pursue Picaro? Could he ever really get away, or was it just a matter of time before this stalker caught him?

Doubt returned him to a greater fear, a hybrid fear that intensified the angers. These led to awful anxieties and deeper doubts. The vicious circle heightened his resolve to resist the evil Hunter's sport. He clenched his fist and solidified his determination to escape the vile hound. As in each of the nights he had outrun the Other, he would do so again. The game was the same, only the *It* was different. He was Picaro. He chastised himself for getting so worked-up and self-provoked. What put him in such a state where fear, anger and doubt surfaced so quickly? The answer was a card handed to him by a man. Picaro examined the card again. When he turned it over, he saw something was written on the other side.

```
A cry goes out, "No Agnus Dei,
Nor that ancient old creed that we say."
    The Kyrie's thrown out,
      "Sophia!" they shout,
And ecclesicrats chant their "Okay."
```

After his lunch, the young man --

"Mr. Old One, please, wait a second," interrupted Ellen, "what is an *Agnus Dei* ?"

He replied, "Not *an Agnus Dei* Ellen, but *the Agnus Dei*."

"Okay, Old One, sir, it is the special day. But what kind of day is it? Some special day like Christmas Day?"

"What? Oh yes, very much so, young lady. You have spoken quite well," said the old man amidst a chuckle.

"Okay, but what is it?"

He answered her question and the ponderings of the other children, "Not an *it*. Rather the *he*."

CHAPTER 8

RETURN TO THE HOLY PLACE

After the noon meal, Chris asked Gerrie to help her look up some words in the dictionary. They found *peavey* and *Kyrie* but not *Agnes Day*. Gerrie said it might be the proper name of a boat and would not be in the dictionary. Grandma smiled and told them to use the large dictionary that included foreign words and phrases. Chris put the small, pocket dictionary back while Gerrie located grandpa's large, old dictionary. They began the search and soon had the answer. They shared the good news with the others.

That afternoon the children congregated at the feet of the old man.

Kay petitioned him, "Old One sir, may we hear more of the story?"

"Yes, but where were we?"

Kay answered, "Picaro had just read the back of the card."

The old man asked, "Which card?"

Several answered in union, "The *Agnus Dei* card."

"Oh yes."

Thus did the frail old man continue the story.

Picaro put the card in his pocket and finished the bread and cheese. After his lunch, the young man walked in the direction of the tall, domed structure. The building rose from the shrubbery as Picaro walked on the rough, flat stones of the narrow pathway. His feet brushed the damp, green moss and lush ferns bordering

54

the walkway. The pathway ended at the raised, rock-paved courtyard which, if any higher, would have been considered an outdoor dais. Picaro noted the wooden doors. The height of the solid fir doors was six times their width. The massive black iron handles located at shoulder height beckoned to him and seeing neither sign forbidding his entrance nor a notice concerning times of visitation, he continued.

Anticipating a locked door, Picaro jerked the right handle. The door cracked and opened. He was mildly surprised, not only initially that it opened, but that it swung with ease on silent hinges. He noticed the excellent quality of the wood as well as the craftsmanship of the work and installation.

Picaro could not determine if the darkness from within poured out or if it consumed the light of day. The young man immediately sensed this to be the sort of place that the Other of his home would inhabit. Most certainly an *It* resided within. He even envisioned the Hunter quietly awaiting the prey to enter the domed building, perhaps even restraining the hound at that very moment. A single pounce by the hound would make the young man a captive and the Hunter's victim. The darkness and the unknown inside the doors disturbed him. Even standing outside with one door open unnerved Picaro. The instant after deciding to shut the giant portal and the moment before the closing commenced, a man appeared in the doorway.

"You are invited to come in," he said.

Startled and taken back, Picaro said, "No, no thank you." Attempting to regain his composure, he explained, "Just curious. Really, I didn't really think the door would open when I pulled the handle."

"My name is Octavos Theist. I am the overseer here in the Holy Place of Woods Town. Please, you are most welcome here and invited to come in."

"No thanks. I am passing through and my curiosity got the best of me. There's no need for me to enter into your holy place."

"This is most certainly not mine. I own nothing. I am only the overseer. But you, my dear friend, are a traveler, one just passing through, a sojourner perhaps? The path you have taken leads, not out of town, but to this holy place. Curiosity may not be the only reason you are here. You are a seeker."

"A seeker? No, really, it was curiosity. I am from ... from the deep woods to the north. I never knew that a holy place like this even existed."

"True, but you did not know it was a holy place until I told you." His voice changed from slight confrontation to warm invitation. "Please, my friend, you can come inside and if you do, you may leave anytime you desire. A great shame it would be, indeed, if a traveler, an explorer, an adventurer such as yourself would be so close to a holy place and did not accept the invitation to enter this place and be within its walls. I feel. I think. I believe. Oh young man, I am certain, that before you got to the edge of town, you would regret the missed opportunity. Now you could go ahead and make that walk to the edge of town. But then you would think for a minute, have a twinge of regret, turn around and return here for a look inside. Or, you might choose to enter now. It's all about choice."

Picaro agreed with the overseer. It would be a shame not to get a look inside. "Okay, but only for a moment."

The young man took several steps inside and the overseer closed the door behind him. Instantly, the darkness descended on him and along with the immersion a feeling of being craved by another. Picaro jerked in panic as he acted on his anxiety and regret.

The commanding voice of the overseer sent a chill through him, "Do not move."

Picaro pivoted and took three striding steps to the door. His right shoulder and eye encountered the door in two steps. Running into the door knocked him to a sitting position with his upper body leaning on his arms.

The voice in the dark sounded again, "Are you badly injured?"

"No," Picaro replied without certainty, "I'm okay."

"Didn't you hear me tell you not to move? You must remain still for a few moments after entering the holy place. Your eyes need to adjust to the darkness of this room. Once you do that, it will be safe to move around. Please, sit there for a few minutes."

Picaro remained seated, not only to allow his eyes the time necessary to adjust but also to determine if he had cut his eye or head. He determined that he had no major injuries. His eyes slowly began to see things. First he noticed the area near the three candles and then the indirect light to the far left. A red light flickered at the right, far across the room. Long pews separated him from the area by that distant red light. The curved pews, also a work of art, were arranged in concentric circles around a point in the floor near the center of the room. There was no ceiling and the dim light from the candles evaporated into the vaulted space.

The overseer spoke, "Do you have any questions?"

"What is this place for?"

Octavos explained, "The Holy Place of Woods Town seeks to serve the various spiritual needs of all peoples according to their personal desires. What does your soul need? What does your spirit desire?"

"I never thought about it. How are the spiritual needs taken care of?"

"That depends on the spiritual system you are under. Which one influences you?"

Picaro replied, "I don't really know what you're talking about."

"Well, do you entone with the Sirens of Sophia, or are you channeling under the Spell of the Trumpeter? Perhaps you are a skeptic communing with the Peering Monocle, or you finger-think with the Auto-Seekers. Maybe you are being pursued by The Hunter, or, --

"Wait," Picaro interrupted before he thought. He hesitated a moment thinking he ought to avoid any discussion about the Hunter.

The overseer looked up and asked, "Yes?"

"Well, you see, I have just escaped from the Other and its territory. I have traveled a great distance to arrive here at Woods Town. How far south does the territory of the Hunter extend?"

Octavos studied the young man. "You are a strange boy. Tell me of the Other. I have not heard of this One."

Picaro tried to change the subject, "The Other is nothing compared to the Hunter. I believe that the Hunter's hound is pursuing me at this very moment."

The Overseer kept his eyes on Picaro, turned his head slightly and called over his shoulder, "Dear!"

A moment later a woman approached from the area of the indirect lighting. "Yes?"

Octavos spoke, "My dear, I would like you to meet, well, I'm sorry, I don't know your name, young man."

"Picaro."

"Yes, Mr. Picaro. This is my wife, Polly. She and I are overseers of services and guardians of the various sacred books."

"Pleased to meet you, ma'am."

"My dear, Mr. Picaro tells me that he has recently escaped from the ... the Other. What do you know of the Other?"

Polly studied Picaro carefully before speaking and began with a calculated inquisition. "The Other. Of the many Ones on record here as well as in my personal studies, there is no reference to the Other. Where have you come from?

Again Picaro wanted to change the subject but knew that he couldn't. "Oh, from the deep woods to the north."

Polly continued, "How long have you lived there."

"All my life."

"And you left there, quite recently, didn't you?"

Before he realized what the consequences were, Picaro answered, "Yes, this morning."

She continued, "Six hours of travel from the deep woods to the north? You must be from the area of Upper Woods. The Other must be your personal One. Am I correct?"

Picaro said, "My personal One? What do you mean?"

"No one else knows of the Other. It is One from your own thinking, a natural conjuring. Am I correct? Young man, you are rather spiritual, but you knew that already."

She pressured him and he sought to stop the conversation. "I have escaped from the Other. I am now being pursued by the Hunter. What can you tell me of the Hunter?"

Octavos raised his voice, "No doubt you have just met one of those fools who sits outside holy places. They try to make people think that there is only one One, the Hunter. They hand out their cards as they attempt to turn holy places like this back to what they once were. These people are narrow-minded, intolerant and unloving."

Polly spoke, "Octavos, I am going to get one of the books of the sacred record."

She left and went to the area where the indirect light originated. Picaro did not want to return to the subject of the Other. His next question, formed in haste, did not accomplish his intent.

"Sir, what did you mean when you said they wanted to turn this holy place back to what it once was?"

Octavos replied with intense conviction, "In times past, this holy place was only for those who worshiped the Hunter. Slowly, open-minded people brought in other Ones. With the help of such people, my wife and I have done this here. At first, people only complained about our teachings and activities. We were not well-received. As time passed, many oppressed us with great opposition and as a result we suffered much. Still, we continued. With a little progress here and some compromise there, we gained a place in the assembly. Our greatest advancements began when we started giving the people what they wanted. Polly and I created and fashioned Ones to the likings of the individual. Once we created other followings in the assembly, then those of the Hunter became another one of the groups, or if you will, rather assimilated."

Just as it is for you children, this was all rather boring for Picaro. He cared nothing about any of this. The young man breathed a sigh of relief when Polly returned, but his respite lasted only a moment. She carried a large book and began speaking as she approached the two men.

"I had a hunch and it paid off. I thought there might be something entered in our record books 15 to 20 years ago. I looked in one of the sacred record books of the activities of the Hunter. Sure enough, it happened here. Picaro had his name cast into the firmament and heard the Thrice Calling of the Echo."

"I did not. I have never been in this place."

Polly contradicted him, "Yes you were, once. You were too young to remember it, only an infant. But it did happen and you were here. Eliza and Mac are your parents and brought you here. Leonhardt the Bishop conducted the Thrice Calling."

Octavos spoke in bitterness, "That man! Leonhardt the Bishop was the biggest obstacle we had to overcome in this holy place. He would not budge in doctrine. There was no compromise in practice with him. He resisted every attempt to introduce another One to the assembly. What vileness wells up from within when I think of the effort, sacrifice and pain we endured to get that man removed from his office in this holy place!"

"Look," said Picaro seizing the moment, "it's not going to take much to remove me from this holy place. Good-by."

Polly took control. "Octavos, you need to calm your spirit. Why not let the water run over the fountain rocks in the back garden? Maybe listening to the relaxing sound and reciting the Sixteen Rules of Arius' Calming will quiet your soul."

As the guardian left, Picaro opened one of the large doors. Polly followed him and spoke in an intense whisper, "You should return to the deep woods of the north. Yes, Picaro, go back to the Other."

The young man replied in a confident voice, "I will not. I am not afraid of the Hunter."

Polly looked about as if someone were trying to listen to her reply. Her eyes flashed about as if she were filled with great fear. Then she said in a potent whisper, "Picaro, you should be."

"No!"

She whispered again, "Then run, Picaro. Run! For the Hunter's hound is after you. You may not rest. Listen carefully to the wind. When it carries the baying of the hound, you must run. Even when the hound tracks you down and stands over you and his windy mouth is breathing on you, run! You may resist the beast even at that point. Remember Picaro, resist and run! Within you, within yourself, you have the power to resist."

He stared at her for a moment and stepped outside the door. He turned and asked, "Do you believe all this stuff about the Hunter?"

Both the stature of her face and the volume of her voice changed, "No!" Her answer coincided with the gavel-like sound of the massive door shutting.

CHAPTER 9

NO ONE'S HERE

Picaro sighed in relief to be outside and away from the holy place. A quick glance along the path gave no indication of Jerome the Kantor's presence. Above the canopy of the trees, a dark cloud covered the sun. A cool gust of wind filtered through the evergreens. The breeze chilled Picaro and gave him goosebumps. Picaro thought he heard the faint baying of a hound in the wind and he turned his head slightly to determine the source of the haunting sound. Hearing nothing more, he dismissed it as the power of suggestion.

The young man quickened the pace in his return to the busy part of town knowing that the noise and bustle of the people would mask both a dark wind that might be felt or any baying hound that might be heard. He was especially thankful to make it without meeting Jerome the Kantor and wondered what it meant to be thankful or to whom thanks ought to be offered.

Picaro resolved to leave Woods Town quickly, rationalizing that there were many other places to visit and he certainly would not have time for all of them. He neither desired nor saw the need to remain in Woods Town. With renewed determination, he found and followed the main road to the south.

Within the hour Picaro was enjoying a leisure hike through a large stand of old growth fir. The thick, dense treetops blocked the sunlight and prevented most underbrush from growing. The fir needles carpeted the forest floor and an occasional white trillium ventured forth as a bearing-beacon for a traveler or a foot light for some untrod path. Picaro left the trail to walk a parallel course amongst the ancient trees, always as his habit dictated, staying within sight of the way. He walked another hour passing through the dense woods and into an open area overlooking a green valley. He paused to enjoy the view and consider his journey, noting with satisfaction that he had never been this far south. He reasoned that Bad Spirit River, miles to his right, continued cascading in its journey to the sea. Ahead of him, on his intended course, Picaro saw another town nestled at the bottom of the valley. The path he chose, as far as he could determine, led to that town.

Four hours later he approached the hamlet and in doing so observed a group of teenagers standing at the side of the old road and pointing to something or someone a short distance from them. Though Picaro drew near, the young people seemed not to notice him. He stopped and blended with the small crowd.

Quietly and with nervous expectation, the young men and women stood watching an open cave. Several of them covered their mouths with their hands in order to suppress a cry of terror or an outburst of laughter. Picaro didn't know what to expect. An older youth who had been near the entrance of the cave returned quickly to the others on the road. He had placed a crudely painted wooden sign near the mouth of the cave.

Picaro whispered to a young man, "What's going on?"

"Shhh," he replied in a whisper, "wait and see."

Here is where Picaro made a mistake. He waited and became an innocent bystander who was blamed for something he did not do.

One young man cued the others to get ready and shortly thereafter he took a branch about the diameter and length of his forearm and threw it into the darkness of the cave. They heard the crashing sound of breaking glass immediately followed by the loud shouts of an angry man. An older man stormed out of the cave. The bedraggled man, an eye patch over one eye, trained his other eye on the teenagers. He waved the stick above his head, shook his free hand, now in the form of a clenched fist, and demanded, "Who threw this into my cave?"

The members of the gang laughed and suddenly pointed to Picaro, declaring, "He did!"

Picaro blurted out, "What? Wait!"

The man read the sign and shook with disgust and anger. With his head turned slightly in order to make efficient use of his good eye, he stared at Picaro and asked, "And did you also put this sign here?"

Before Picaro could deny it, the others chanted, "Yes, he did! He did it!"

Another counseled, "Your eye ... keep your eye on him."

They jostled and forced Picaro in the direction of the man and their pushing caused Picaro the accused to fall at the feet of the livid man. The crowd of teenagers dispersed, running in the direction of the town, laughing and cavorting as they escaped. Before Picaro could make a move to get away, the one-eyed man spoke, "You budge an inch and I'll brain you with this tree limb."

Picaro thought about a quick escape but decided against the attempt. He was on his hands and knees in front of the man and in addition, his pack caused an imbalance and made him feel awkward. He did not think he could accomplish his flight without taking a severe blow to the head. Consequently, he remained still.

The agitated man spoke again, "Did you throw this stick into my cave?"

Picaro answered, "Would you believe me if I said *no* ?"

With the hint of a smile, the man replied, "If our places were switched and you were in my place, would you believe me?"

Picaro grinned, "I asked first."

The man grinned even wider, "I have the stick."

"Okay, I'm not sure I would believe you."

"Well spoken. Very good. So if nothing else young man, at least you seem honest."

"Or, sufficiently deceitful to fool you."

The man guffawed. He moved back and lowered his weapon, speaking as he did, "You may stand. I will not harm you. I know that you did not do it."

Picaro asked, "How are you able to know I didn't throw the stick into your cave?"

"Excellent! In fact," continued the one-eyed man, "please accept my apology for even thinking that you were the guilty person."

Picaro wondered and asked, "What makes you so certain?"

"You. Use your head, boy. I've never you seen before. I have seen the rest of those over-grown juvenile delinquents often enough. In addition, it is obvious to me that you have some sort of education. Those others dropped out of school and know neither spelling nor grammar. Take a look at that homemade sign of theirs."

The young man read the sign out loud, "*Aunti Theist.* It would make me angry to be called *aunti* too. But it's really not that big a deal, is it? I mean, I'd be more angry because of the damage done by that stick than being called a woman."

"What?" asked the cave-dweller.

"What do you mean, what? Did they spell your name incorrectly? Is the proper name, Theist, spelled wrong?"

"No," he responded with indignant frustration, "that is correct. Look at the word before it. They spelled it A-u-n-t-i. Not

65

only have they spelled that incorrectly, but they used the wrong word in the first place. Besides, it's a prefix, not a word."

The younger man confessed, "I don't understand."

"Look, because of my beliefs and this cave, the people around here don't think much of me. So they call me Anti Theist. But they got it wrong. It should not be *Anti*. It should be *A*."

Picaro waited. Finally he spoke, "It should be a what?"

Further agitated, he replied in a loud voice, "It should be *A*. Just *A*. If they knew what they were talking about, they would simply call me Atheist."

Picaro did not reply. He was not sure what to say or how to respond. He wondered if he ought not change the subject. Something flashed into his mind. "Are you related to Octavos Theist, the guardian of the holy place in Woods Town?"

"You have not been paying attention. I told you that Anti Theist was the name given to me by the people of the town, though those delinquents now seem to find it humorous to call me Aunti Theist. But my name is neither Anti Theist nor A Theist, though I will admit the latter describes me. So no, I am not related to any superstitious guardian in Woods Town or anywhere else. And I have nothing to do with any holy place or the ones they worship."

Picaro asked, "Does this territory belong to the Hunter or to the Other?"

The older man squinted his lone eye and spoke with disgust, "The Hunter? Do not speak the name of that mythical, non-existent one to me. That one, along with the Voice Within, the Seven Spirits of the Grove and the Arch-Siren, do not exist. They are all dehydrated fog."

"What about the Other? Have you heard the myth of the Other?"

"No, and I have no desire to listen to fairy tales. What? Is the Other something you dreamed up?"

Picaro replied quickly, "No, I once heard someone mention the Other, that's all. Tell me the name of the One you worship. Which One is it?"

His chest rose with a deep breath and he spoke in firm conviction, "I worship no one."

"Know-One? Did Know-One catch you?"

"Right, no one caught me."

"Do you worship Know-One?"

"Yes."

"Know-One makes you do it?"

"That's correct, no one makes me worship."

"Is that why you live in this cave?"

"Yes."

"Does Know-One care that you live in this cave?"

"No one cares. Oh like today, I am bothered once in awhile, but I understand. I don't like it, but I understand."

"Know-One bothers you?"

"Like I said, once in a while."

"Do you like it when Know-One gives you a bad time?"

"As you might imagine, I prefer it?"

"You prefer it?!"

"Sure I do!"

"Is this Know-One's cave?"

"It's my cave."

"And Know-One doesn't care."

"Mind your grammar, boy. You used a double negative. I already told you, no one cares."

"So, Know-One does care."

"Alright, that's better."

"Is Know-One in the cave?"

"No one is in the cave."

"Know-One is in there?"

"Look, I am out here with you aren't I? I live with no one and I am married to no one. So, my friend, no one is in the cave."

"You are married to Know-One! I never heard of such a thing. Is it even possible?"

"It is not only possible, but I prefer it?"

"Is Know-One in your cave at this very moment?"

"Yes, young man, no one is in there."

"If I went in there right now, I would find Know-One?"

"Absolutely. Look, if you want, I will take you in and show you that no one is there."

Picaro shivered. "No, I believe you. Know-One is in there. Please tell me, is Know-One pursuing me?"

"How would I know? But let me give you some advice and counsel. As you travel these roads, especially in the isolated areas, beware. Being pursued, getting caught and suffering is a distinct possibility. Look, you seem like a decent enough fellow and even though a tad weird, I would hate to see you get hurt. So look, as far as I am able to tell, no one is after you right now."

Visibly shaken, Picaro glanced around quickly. He decided to get away while he had the opportunity.

"I must be on my way right now, immediately. Thank you for letting me know about Know-One."

The one-eyed man tilted his head in dismay and silently wondered about the young man.

Picaro took a couple of steps and stopped. He had one final question. He turned around and asked, "You said that A Theist is not your name. Would you mind telling me what your real name is?"

"Not at all," replied the man as he stood in front of his cave, "my name is Paul E. Feemos."

Picaro left and as he did, he thought he heard Paul say something. He wasn't certain, but it sounded something like, "I'll be in shortly."

Picaro ran.

CHAPTER 10

MOONLIGHT TEARS

"Let me recall how it goes, children. The words are from an ancient work called *The Rubiayat*. I memorized parts of it long ago. Oh yes."

The moving finger writes; and, having writ, moves on:
Nor all your piety
Nor wit shall lure it back to cancel half a line,
Nor all your tears wash out a word of it.

"Do you understand, little ones? Are you able to cipher its truth and meaning?"

"No," several spoke in unison.

"So be it," the old man replied. "You will. You have a lifetime to think on these things. A lifetime."

Whether thinking on these things or perplexed at the old man's manner of speaking or unable to formulate words, the five cousins continued to listen.

"Dear children, imagine. Imagine ... though I do not think you have to imagine at all, for you have all dreamed the dream, haven't you?"

His question received no answer.

"Imagine running, and though not being caught, you are being pursued by the hound. Each day you run. Each day you know that it is behind you. You feel the presence. Each night you run. Each night you hear the hound in the shadows. You sense it.

And there is evening and there is morning, one day. You continually cross a great chasm on a flimsy footbridge that spans the yawning abyss. The unrelenting padding of the hound's paws behind you release the once-trod treads causing them to fall and disappear into the grim mists that silently swallow the 24 and 7."

> *Whether at Naishapur or Babylon,*
> *Whether the Cup with sweet or bitter run,*
> > *The Wine of Life keeps oozing drop by drop,*
> > *The Leaves of Life keep falling one by one.*

"This is kinda scary," one of the children confessed.

"Yea," agreed another, "more scary than witches, trolls and hob-goblins."

The old man asked, "Why more scary?"

"Because, sir, your story sounds real," admitted one of the cousins.

The teller of the story asked, "And trolls are not real?"

"No. I mean, they're not, are they?"

The children looked to the old man who, after a moment deep in contemplation, sighed.

Mick suggested, "Can we go back to our story."

"Yes," the others replied with enthusiasm.

"No," countered the old man.

"What?" asked Mick with disappointment. "Why must the story stop now?"

The story-teller spoke softly, "There's no going back to the story and no stopping it. There is no standing still. At cock crow one chasm has been crossed and is left behind. Another begins. There is no choice. Though one crawls on all fours, hobbles along with a walking-stick or dances in the prime of this world's life, the race is run. So Mick, we can not go back to our story and we can not stand still."

Picaro ran until he no longer saw the bend in the road by Know-One's cave. The cycle of fear from anger to doubt to fear continued as it had so often. He sought a way to keep from being in the area this night. The alternative was to sleep in the woods, something he dreaded. For the first time, he considered that his life with the Other had not been so terrible. Though only hours from his home, he was pursued by several invisible stalkers.

He thought on the events that beset him as he arrived at the town he had seen earlier, a village about the same size as Woods Town. Numerous cedars grew in this lowland and appropriately the pioneers had given the place a name, Cedarville. An impressive shake mill provided the locals with employment, either working in the mill or cutting shake bolts in the woods.

A tall, black-haired man greeted Picaro as he entered the main roadway through town. The tall man nodded his head to Picaro and extended his right hand. Picaro smiled and shook his hand just as the man's left hand slapped him on the back. When Picaro brought his right hand back, he held a small card.

> ```
> I am Alvin the Absolver from the
>   ancient village of Benedicamus
>    at the base of High Mountain.
>       I may not speak to you.
>    (Please return this card to me
>        after you have read it.)
> ```

Picaro pitched the card to the ground and snarled at Alvin the Absolver. In a loud voice and with a wrathful, exaggerated expression, he backed away and shouted, "Leave me alone! I don't want any of your cards!"

Before permitting Alvin the Absolver either enough time or further opportunity to give him another card, the young man turned and tromped away. His anger continued to control and direct him as he staccato-stepped along the main roadway of Cedarville. Less than twelve hours had passed since he waved good-bye to his mother and touched his brothers last as the custom dictated. To him it seemed a lifetime ago and a great chasm separated him from his past. He could not go back.

A few minutes later he raised his stormy eyes and saw a scuffle ahead. Though not in a mood to be concerned and willing not to become involved, the screaming of a young boy or girl moved him to take notice. In front of a store several buildings from Picaro's position, a scuffle was taking place and from within the huddle Picaro heard the cries. As he approached, he saw a small boy being taunted and bullied by three or four older boys. This was not Picaro's concern until he recognized the bullies were several of the same young people who tricked him at the cave.

Picaro and his brothers had done their share of fighting, usually against one other. No rules governed such fights and Picaro's eye still bore the scar where green bark from alder slab wood had been thrown by Dave and had found its mark. In another encounter, the oldest brother's arm had been stabbed with a table fork when he tried to take food from Anton's plate. Four tiny scars still testify to that brotherly skirmish. However, if someone attacked one of the three brothers, he quickly found two others joined in the battle.

Picaro started an undetected approach on the group of young men, an approach that increased in speed and momentum. As he ran, his left arm slipped from his backpack. He let the pack fall from his shoulder to the crook of his elbow and then slide to his right hand. As he came upon the bullies, Picaro jumped, shouted and swung the pack around with his right hand. The backpack knocked one teenager to his hands and knees. Picaro's left shoulder slammed into another and sent him sprawling to the ground. Caught off guard by the suddenness of the attack, the boldness of the intercessor, his tenorized holler and their two stunned comrades, the remaining bullies turned and ran. The two on the ground scrambled to their feet and joined the others in flight.

The young man lifted the boy from the dusty road as the latter struggled to hold back the tears that pooled in his eyes. Picaro avoided a direct look into the boy's eyes, knowing that such contact would cause the boy to cry. He spoke in an understanding manner as he brushed the dirt and debris from the boy's clothing and hair.

"Hey buddy, it looks like you took on a fairly sizeable crowd. You sure seemed to be holding your own. I hope you didn't mind me coming to reduce the odds?"

While the little boy did not speak, his eyes expressed appreciation for his intercessor, although as I said, Picaro did not look directly into them.

Picaro focused his attention to the non-existent dirt on the boy's back, brushing it off with his hands, "We took care of those guys didn't we?"

"Yea," came his snubbed answer.

Sensing calmness and control from the boy's response, Picaro extended his hand and continued leading the conversation, "My name is Picaro. What's the name of my fighting buddy?"

They shook hands and the boy answered, "Manoah."

"Well, Manoah, where you headed?"

The boy shot a glance in the direction that the rowdy crowd had gone.

Picaro understood and spoke, "You know I'm headed in that direction. Maybe you'd let me walk along with you for a ways?"

An expression of relief formed on Manoah's face and he answered, "Sure. My mother wanted me to deliver a sack to the dry goods store. I was on my way back when those older guys saw me and began chasing me. I tried to get away, but they ran faster and caught me. Maybe you'd like to walk with me to my house and meet my family?"

Picaro also understood that Manoah wanted protection and companionship until he got home and for these reasons, accepted the invitation, "Well why not, if it's in that general direction? I believe I'd enjoy the company. Manoah, you lead and I'll follow."

The boy led him to the southeast corner of town and took a side path to the northeast. They did not see the bullies as they walked the mile to Manoah's home. The house had been built where the woods gave way to open fields. Two small sheds and a crude barn screened the house from the forest. The one story house was obviously small for the family of five and they gathered within for meals, evening table talk and sleeping. Manoah's oldest sister worked in town during the day and did chores at home before and after. His other sister helped her mother at home. Manoah's parents worked a small farm with a couple of cows and a dozen chickens. The family recently planted a vegetable garden in the field to the east of the house.

The two arrived in time for a quick tour of the place and the evening meal. Manoah introduced Picaro to the family and told them that they had been attacked by those Cedarville hoodlums who had been bothering people. Together he and Picaro stood up to them and sent the lot of them off in short order. Picaro gave a slight smile that did not go by unnoticed by Manoah's father. The family invited the guest to sup the evening meal with them and gave no opportunity for him to turn it down. Manoah's mother set a place next to her son. The head of the family moved to the head of the table. Prominently displayed behind him on the wall hung a large iron trap. Picaro noticed the interior walls, the furniture as well as the other furnishings and mentally concluded that Manoah's father was a craftsman of and with wood.

Manoah's mother placed a heavy metal kettle half full of poor-man's stew on the table. The man sitting at the head of the table led his family in a prayer to the Hunter and ended the prayer of thanksgiving "in the name of the hound." Picaro stiffened and his defenses heightened. He wanted to leave, but forced himself to remain. The stew invited him to stay and the hospitality beckoned him to eat. Manoah's mother served Picaro first, filling his bowl with the hand-carved, wooden ladle. The guest noticed that the others received smaller portions of the poor-man's stew. Homemade bread, hand-churned butter and canned, blackberry jam completed the meal. Whoever set the table had given Picaro the largest glass and the sister who poured his milk filled his glass. After eating, they continued to talk at the crowded table.

Manoah's mother asked, "Picaro, where are you from?"

"I am from the deep woods to the north, beyond Woods Town and Upper Woods."

"Are you traveling alone?"

With youthful confidence he answered, "Yes, very much alone. I need no one. I mean, I don't need anyone."

She continued, "Are you going somewhere in particular?"

"Not anywhere that I know. I mean not anywhere that I've been. I heard there is a war and I am going to the war to become a warrior. So, wherever the war is, well, that's where I'm going."

Manoah responded quickly informing his family, "Really, he already is a mighty warrior! You should have seen him with that Cedarville bunch."

Picaro's appearance hinted at a blush. He smiled and said, "I was only half of the fighting force. I had a warrior friend at my side."

Manoah's face revealed both admiration for the warrior and personal pride.

The father who had listened without expression of interest or surprise, spoke to Picaro, "What, exactly, does a warrior do?"

"Well sir, I'm not altogether certain. I mean, it's obvious there is a lot of fighting to be done. There are a great many battles to be waged. In fact, just thinking about it makes me want to get there all the sooner. I don't want to miss anything. You don't think the fighting will be over before I get there, do you?"

Manoah's mother said in a calm but mournful tone, a manner as if recalling a time long ago and a hurt deep within, "No, there will always be wars and rumors of wars. The young and strong go to fight and many of them die. A sister loses a brother and her children never know their uncle. A young woman ages a decade when told she is a war-widow. Mothers and fathers receive the news and grieve until they enter their graves. Each one awakens in the darkness of shadowy nights and sheds soul-rending tears that glisten in the moonlight."

No one spoke for a moment and the silence became uncomfortable.

The woman's voice changed, "Manoah, you will need to make up a place for yourself to sleep. Our guest will be using your bed tonight."

Before the young boy could respond, Picaro spoke with firmness, "Thank you, but that will not be necessary. I do not wish to impose on you."

The father said, "There are only a few hours until sunset. You won't be able to get very far before you have to find a place to sleep. Please stay the night with us. It's no imposition."

"No, I will not stay in your house. You do have a couple of sheds outside. May I sleep in one of them?"

Manoah's mother spoke with indignation, "I will not have you sleeping out there."

Picaro said, "If you will not let me sleep in one of your sheds, then I must leave."

The father announced, "You may sleep in one of the sheds, but I do not suggest the chicken coop. The wood shed may be most uncomfortable. You should be able to get some sleep in the animal shelter. Would you sleep there, Picaro?"

"Yes, thank you."

He looked at his son and continued, "You need to clean out the corner stall and put down some fresh straw. Take out one of your blankets for him."

Manoah did as told. The others rose from the table to attend to evening chores. Picaro followed the boy to the barn. As they made a place for sleeping in the corner stall, they talked about far-away lands and other battles.

Just before dark, Manoah's mother came to the barn with a light in her hand. Already knowing the answer to the question, she asked Picaro, "You will not break the fast with us in the morning, will you?"

He answered, "No, I'll be leaving early."

"Then don't forget to take this with you." She hung a cloth sack on a peg. "Manoah, say good-bye to Picaro and come into the house. It's getting late. Picaro, I will remember you and your parents in my nightly supplications. Good night and good-bye."

He said, "Please, you need only remember my mother."

"Only your mother?"

"Yes, you don't need to remember my father."

"And what about you, young Picaro? What of you? Should I include you in my tear-glistened prayers?"

She left without giving him an opportunity to reply. It didn't matter, for Picaro did not know what to say.

A few minutes later, Picaro rested alone in the dark. He positioned his pack as a pillow and pulled the blanket over him. As his head came down on the pillow something poked him below his right eye. He supposed it to be a piece of straw and sought to locate it with his hand. He discovered a small piece of paper and instantly knew it was a card from Alvin the Absolver. He had slipped it into Picaro's pack when he slapped him on the back.

Picaro did not want to read it, but knew that he would. A beam of moonlight came through one spot on the wall of the barn. He held the card in the moon's beam and read it.

> *The execs cry, "Attendance is falling!*
> *And pastor you need a new calling!*
>   *So pick up thy staff,*
>   *And break it in half.*
> *Law-Gospel is now quite a-Pauline."*

While this meant nothing to Picaro, he knew what was written on the other side. Nevertheless he turned the card over and read it. These words meant something to him.

> *The Hunter is after you.*
> *The Wind has given your scent*
>   *to His Hound.*
> *At this very moment*
> *His Hound is tracking you.*

Something outside the barn cast a shadow blocking the light from the moonbeam for an instant. The moonlight returned. Picaro froze. He reasoned that it must have been a passing cloud. The shadow was cast again, only for a second. He listened to the wind. A sudden gust blew into the trees causing a large limb to cast the shifting shadows once more.

Picaro put his head on the pillow and pulled the blanket over his head. He hated the Hunter. In the midst of the wind, he heard the howl of the hound. His lips cursed the hound. Under the cover of darkness and with the moon casting shadowy shapes on the blanket, Picaro wept. The tears came from one quite lonely and filled with big fear.

CHAPTER 11

FRIENDS IN BATTLE

When a large river collides with an ocean there is a great churning of forces. The river, fed by the spring runoff of high mountains, penetrates deeply into the ocean. The juggernaut of water is not to be denied as it slithers down its path. The massive ocean, while suffering a setback, is not defeated. As the tide rises wave after wave pushes saltwater up the river's mouth. The contest continues unabated until the day of the great undoing. Neither ocean nor river is completely victorious or totally defeated.

"Sir," interrupted Mick as gently as possible, "is this part of the same story?"

"Yes," answered the old man. He hesitated and added, "Perhaps I am getting too far afield?"

"I don't know. I was just trying to follow what you were saying. I do want to hear the story and understand."

"Okay Mick, I'll be more direct."

The war was fought between two evenly matched armies, all designed and equipped to win but never conquer, to lose but avoid destruction. The Side of the Sun fought and won the day while the Forces of the Dark One fought and ruled the night. Two battles raged every 24 hours. The battle at dusk turned in favor of the Dark One as its fighting demons overcame the Side of the Sun. At the dawn of each day, the warriors of the Sun arose to defeat the Forces of the Dark One. The site changed as the foundation of any battleground is capable of withstanding only so much destruction, war and rubble. For quality warfare, combatants need a clean field, new buildings and additional innocent victims.

Picaro placed his name in the pool of potential warriors. When the lots were drawn, his came up for the Side of the Sun. Two years after pledging as a warrior, he waited for his first combat. The only way to be called up for battle was when a warrior fell in combat. It was also possible if one of the warriors "fulfilled the sevens," a rare accomplishment. When the casualties of war increased, the number of those called up as replacements increased. Each warrior waited his turn and worked as he waited. Thus Picaro spent every battle in support - lifting, stacking, piling, supplying and moving. He grumbled about his activities not being different from his old days at the sawmill.

After the four-day Battle of Two Towns, when many combatants on both sides drowned in the quickly rising flood waters, Picaro received his summons. When his call came, he dropped the fifty pound sack of corn from his shoulder and the kernels poured from the split sack. Without looking back, he ordered the envious others to clean up the mess.

Two days later, the new warrior was equipped with fighting gear and weapon. He had orders to walk to the dry region southwest of Two Towns. With excited determination, he quick-marched the twenty miles to the war zone. There he waited, a mere half day's hike from the battleground. It was truly a brief time and a short distance when compared to the 1200-mile, two-month journey south from The Dell.

The Battle of Monitor Lizard Plateau would be fought within the week. The organizers chose the new site because it provided opportunity for strategy. The terrain did not lend itself to massive, surprise attacks. This, the organizers hoped, might keep the casualties low and the interest high. Individual strategy, stealth and effort would be required and certainly rewarded in this battle. As new warriors approached the Monitor Lizard Plateau, the overall security tightened and the individual tension increased. The lower-ranking military leaders assigned to the Side of the Sun assembled the warriors in squads of ten. The squad leaders provided minimal orientation and gave numerous orders.

Picaro's squad consisted of five warriors from the eastern nation of Seven Republics, two from South Isle farms, one from a cattle ranch in the land of High Plains and one off a ship. The five easterners were part of a group of eight life-long friends from the city and had joined together. The eight hoped to fight as warriors at each other's side. However when the lots were drawn three received assignments attaching them to the Forces of the Dark One. The random drawings divided the octet and pitted them five against three and three against five.

The leader of the squad spoke. "Let there be silence. You are one mile from the battleground perimeter. The perimeter is defined for you. It is a dry creek bed. Once you cross it you are at war. The terrain is open and rocky, quite similar to what you have seen in the last day or two. There are no trees, but scrub brush and bushes are common. The ground rises steeply to a plateau that is, for now, controlled by the Side of the Sun. As the day light fades, the dusk fighting will begin and the Forces of the Dark One will dominate. Presently they are entrenched below the northern edge of the plateau. As the dark of night deepens, they will drive our warriors back to the southern tip of the plateau. This will take them all night."

The leader stopped and looked at each one of the new warriors.

"No questions? ... Fine. Tonight you cross the perimeter and enter the Battle of Monitor Lizard Plateau. Your primary mission is to report to the commanding field officer for the Side of the Sun. As you make your -"

One of the five interrupted the leader, "Don't we get to fight the Forces of the Dark One?"

The leader roared, "Silence, fool! You will not speak unless given permission."

No one spoke and he continued, "As you make your way to the top of the plateau, the night will begin to give way to the morning light. The battle at dawn will turn in our favor. The Forces of the Dark One will either be destroyed or retreat across the plateau and down the north side. If you encounter any of them retreating, let them know you are a warrior."

"You are a squad, ten members. I am sending you in pairs. You decide who your partner is. The first pair leaves before midnight."

Two pair came from the Seven Republics. The extra easterner joined the sailor. Since the two South Isle farmers paired off immediately, Picaro and the cattle rancher emerged as partners. The cattle rancher's name was Samuel and the two of them talked as they prepared for their departure. These two found they had much in common. Each wanted to get away from home. Each was quiet, strong, reserved and reasonably intelligent. They discussed team and personal strategy for the mission ahead. They agreed to cover one another and think from the other's perspective. Picaro and Samuel had confidence in each other and this made for excellent teamwork.

Although they didn't know it, they both feared the days and especially the nights awaiting them. They kept their private thoughts secret and their doubts and anxiety at bay. At this point in their lives, to confess being afraid amounted to an admission of being a weakling or a coward. They needed to grow older before being able to confess personal fears. Such a maturity, while usually developing gradually and naturally through the years of experience and thoughtful reflection, comes rapidly when young men go to war. These two would learn quickly.

The leaders sent the fourth pair, Samuel and Picaro, on their way at 11:45 pm. They left side by side and began whispering as the distance from the campfire increased and as the still darkness overcame the light. With their eyes adjusted to the night, the light from the moon provided adequate illumination of the desert floor. Soon the two arrived at the edge of the dry creek bed. The tensions increased within. Their whisperings ceased. Their eyes focused on the land stretching beyond them. They walked with their backs slightly arched and their weapons at the ready. Now the moonlight provided too much revelation. They became open targets advancing on the enemy's position.

Picaro moved quickly from bush to bush and using his peripheral vision, monitored his partner's movements. Samuel proceeded in like manner. After an hour of dashing from shadow to shadow, they commenced the incline to the plateau. The scrub brush thinned, now supplanted by the scattered outcropping of rock and large boulders which served as welcome places of cover. They began the ascent, though the incline was not particularly steep. Above them they heard the sounds of battle. Samuel crouched behind a large rock and motioned his fellow warrior to join him.

"We need to talk for a minute," Samuel whispered into Picaro's ear.

"What about?"

"Infiltrating the enemy lines to get to our warriors on the Side of the Sun is extremely dangerous. Isn't it reasonable to think that we will be meeting others coming down in a few minutes?"

Picaro answered, "Yes, I've heard some fighting far above us. Troops will be coming down, especially as the Side of the Sun gets ready for its counter-offense and begins to drive the Forces of the Dark One back at dawn."

"Right, but how will we be able to tell the difference while it is still dark? I mean, it's likely that the first ones coming down will be from the Dark One. And, the last ones we meet will be from the Side of the Sun. But what about those in between? In this darkness we can't tell which ones we will be meeting."

"You're right," Picaro whispered. He thought for a minute and said, "What do you think of this strategy? The first ones coming down will be from the Side of the Dark One. You and I will keep going up until we hear them drawing near our position. When they do, we'll take our places on the downhill side of large rocks like this one. We will be at the same elevation, only about ten feet apart. The first ones down will probably be cowards from the Dark One's side. If they come down one at a time and they are between us then we take care of them. If there's more than one, we let them pass."

Samuel added, "Sounds good to me. This is our first battle and it's sure not a time to be stupid. When one of them comes between us, you or I could get his attention and the other attack from his back."

"Fine. Like you said, the first ones will be cowards who are not looking for a fight. Now, after the first dozen or so we'll have to be careful because those retreating down the hill will be like us - trying to complete their mission and hoping to stay alive. Let's begin our ascent slowly, stopping every ten to twenty feet to listen. Later anyone coming down the hill facing us, we let go by. They will either be the cowards of the enemy or the brave ones on our side. However, if anyone is backing down the hill, then we attack them together, quickly and as quietly as possible."

"Right," concluded Samuel and added, "by the time the first light of dawn arrives everyone we meet will be facing us and we will be able to see when we have infiltrated to the Side of the Sun. But Picaro, we need each other. So let's take our time and not make any mistakes."

"Agreed. Samuel, we're in this together. Let's complete this mission together," Picaro whispered firmly.

The plan worked to perfection. The two warriors took their time and completed their objective. Along the way the enemy suffered from their strategy, patience, teamwork, stealth and skill. The two young men rejoiced in their initial test as warriors. As the team made its way across the sunny plateau in the warmth of the midday sun, there was a sense of accomplishment and fulfillment. They radiated excitement and enthusiasm. Ah, what exhilarating feelings those young men had as they passed through the line!

Great smiles and raucous laughter overflowed as they recounted the events of the night.

Picaro and Samuel were the last to report to the commanding field officer that day, but they did make it. Not all from the squad did. One of the five from the eastern nation of Seven Republics had been lost in the battle. Such losses were expected. Warriors knew this possibility. It was understood. It was a given, and especially a given that this always happens to someone else.

Thus ended Picaro's first day as a warrior. Oh yes, I almost forgot. You remember the warrior from the squad who was killed in battle? Well, he was killed by his long-time friend, the one assigned to the Forces of the Dark One.

CHAPTER 12

A BABY'S PROTECTION

The Battle of Monitor Lizard Plateau continued eight days and nights. As anticipated by the war directors, the casualties on both sides remained relatively light. This allowed for the Forces of the Dark One and the Side of the Sun to return to full strength. Over the next two years, the war moved through the sparsely populated southern region. When the people heard the sounds of war they left until it passed.

Picaro and Samuel followed the same general plan they formed that first night. They listened to the mission objectives, received their orders and met to talk before going into battle. The two warriors planned the work and worked the plan. Though they knew the plan of action and methods of accomplishing it without discussing the details, they discussed the details. They made no assumptions. They covered every step and anticipated various scenarios. With cautious confidence, mutual respect and thoughtful concern for each other, they developed and refined their operations.

One of the more difficult aspects of being a warrior was that of sleep. The ever-shifting tides of battle and the two-a-day skirmishes at dusk and dawn left no time for quality sleep. Noon remained the safest time for sleep on the Side of the Sun, the opposite being true for the enemy. At midnight, when the Side of the Sun hid amidst the shadows, Picaro and Samuel took turns sleeping and watching.

Being a faithful warrior required stamina and dedication, both mentally and physically. The work yielded results no less rewarding than remaining alive. Samuel and Picaro stayed alert and alive, now the only ones from their original squad. True brotherly love grew between them and they knew that to remain among the living each had to trust and rely on the other. They fought battle after battle and campaign after campaign at each other's side.

The more populated the areas, the more dangerous the fighting. Rumors circulated that the three day Battle of Mud Dauber Flats cost more than 2,700 warriors from the Side of the Sun. It happened when the Forces of the Dark One seized the initiative at the dusk skirmish on the second day. A sudden rain storm slowed the retreat of the Side of the Sun and 1600 warriors died during one hour of transitional fighting. The Skeeter Ridge Battle was waged in the town below the steep ridge. Many civilians could not flee the fighting as the town was cut off by the ridge above and the canyon below. While the Forces of the Dark One entrenched at the east, the Side of the Sun closed on their position from the west. The people of the town, unable to escape and unprepared for the onslaught suffered horrendous casualties as they were trapped in the buildings and caught in the cross fire. Civilians fled whenever possible and wherever able, sometimes tragically running directly into the fiercest fighting instead of away from it. These atrocities troubled Picaro and Samuel and began to dampen their enthusiasm for war.

During the dusk retreat of the Side of the Sun one early evening, when Picaro and Samuel ran beside the buildings and through the side streets, they were suddenly confronted and accosted. Their enemy did not startle them as they ran through an alley and around a corner. No indeed, if only that were the case they would have known how to respond.

Rather, a little baby, no longer breathing, remained in the lifeless arms of a young woman, both apparently victims of the fighting. Their lives ended in an alley at the bottom of a set of stairs. It appeared that the woman attempted to flee by going up the stairway and had managed only two steps before she and the baby became victims of the war.

The alley continued to the left with the stairs providing exit to the right. The stairway had some ten steps up to a landing and from the landing another set of steps ascended to the right and disappeared behind a wall. The damaged door at the landing remained unhinged at the bottom and therefore, permanently open. Such a position provided a visual barrier for anyone at the top few stair steps.

Neither Samuel nor Picaro continued their flight. Shock stunned and disbelief paralyzed them. Breathing in loud gasps from their escape seemed an unspoken desecration. The surreal scene called for a sanctified silence in the presence of such stillness. Even the heartbeat of the living mocked the dead. Samuel and Picaro stood on holy ground and they perceived themselves, at best, as intruders. The sensation was not only because of death itself. Obviously, both of the men had seen plenty of death in the last few years. Combatants fell in every battle. The possibility of life coming to an end began when the man stepped forward and answered, in the affirmative, the call to be a warrior. The specter that presented itself before the two men at the foot of the stairs differed from all other expressions of death. The love of the woman for the baby led to her death. She might have made the last eight steps if not weighed down with the baby. However, the evidence bore witness to the truth that she did not consider the infant a regrettable burden. While the corpse of the woman troubled them, the body of the baby shocked them into immobility. Here before them, injustice and innocence met as the selfish wrath of humanity collided with a fresh promise, and a baby gave way having neither choice then nor the breath of life now. The baby in the arms of the woman testified to a life unlived. Both men sensed, knew and understood that life was not meant to be ended in this way. Each man, in his own way, pondered what might be an appropriate death for a baby. They thought of none. Death was not intended for babies. It was not intended at all. It is unnatural and when it confronts as it did with this mother and child there is some form of unraveling that takes place in the heart and soul of the observer.

For the two warriors time seemed neither to pass nor to exist. In reality it did and however long they gazed upon death, it became too long. The sounds of the approaching enemy startled the two numbed soldiers and dictated their response as warriors. The Forces of the Dark One closed on their position in the corner of the alley. Samuel took a stride to continue through the escape alley ahead but stopped short. Ahead the Forces of the Dark One awaited them. At that instant, trapped in a maze of increasing darkness, Picaro believed he would die. With his teeth clenched, he put on the face of a warrior about to give his ultimate. He resolved to make others precede him before he drew his last breath. He backed into the corner of the alley and alongside the stairway. If the enemy wanted him, then they would have to take him head on. Picaro lowered his weapon, leaned forward and waited. He began a low growling and forced saliva through his teeth.

Samuel had similar thoughts, but a way of escape also came to him. He motioned to his friend in an emphatic, mouthed whisper, "No!"

Samuel knew the enemy was near and closing rapidly. He gave his weapon to Picaro and pulled the baby from the woman's arms, noting the limberness of the infant as he did. He stretched the baby out on the left side of the fifth step. He pushed the woman on the first three steps and placed one of her arms toward the baby, giving at first glance, the appearance of a maternal beckoning and after a prolonged look, a reluctant releasing of her offspring. Samuel retrieved his weapon from the nearly weeping Picaro and motioned for his friend to follow. Carefully they negotiated their way alongside the woman, over the tiny baby and up the stairs. Stepping over the baby was difficult for Picaro, conjuring mind-accosting feelings of violation, desecration and abandonment.

Ten steps up from the landing, any further escape ended. Another door, this one locked and bolted from the inside, forced the two warriors into another dead end at the top of the stairs. The sounds of the enemy clarified and intensified as they neared the position of the two soldiers on the Side of the Sun. Picaro and Samuel sat beside each other on the top step. Their backs were to the door and their weapons, like royal scepters, stood at the ready in front of them and between their feet. Although only ten feet from the alley below, they remained hidden from view. From both ends of the alley, enemy warriors converged on the eery scene. The sounds of four warriors gave way and Picaro and Samuel heard only the noise of distant battle. The baby and the woman silenced the four warriors just as it had done to the two a few moments before. The hidden pair remained still and ready to defend themselves. Time seemed to flow in slow motion for them as their minds tried to understand everything. Finally those below spoke and the two above listened.

"Did you encounter two of the enemy coming from this end of the alley?"

"No, you're the first we've met in this long, crooked alley."

"Were there any other alleys branching off from this one?"

"I don't recall. Do you?"

"No, but I am not here to draw maps either. I'm a warrior."

"Not much of one if you can't even remember where you've just been."

"Well spoken. But remember, we aren't the ones who haven't been able to catch up with the enemy. You are. Maybe we can help you find them. Where did you last see them? Are you certain they came up this alley? Perhaps you have been chasing shadows. Shadows don't fight back, do they?"

"Silence, fool!"

"Well, why don't you start looking for them? If I were you I'd begin by going up these stairs. Perhaps they are up there somewhere. Anyway, we have more to do than stand here talking to you."

Samuel and Picaro tensed, each thinking that their presence must be felt by those below.

"Then go do it. I doubt that they went up the stairs. Besides if they did, they'd be long gone by now. Actually, I think it a great possibility that you saw them coming and hid yourself until they got by. No doubt in my mind. You're doing nothing more than running from the battle. You should've been going in the other direction. It's cowards like you that make me seethe, retreating when the rest of our forces are advancing."

"Really? Well perhaps you'd like to find out how much of a coward I am. Why not give me your home address? That way, after I dispatch you I could send a letter to your family letting them know you'd been killed by a lowly coward!"

"Save it for the enemy you are fleeing!"

Picaro and Samuel heard the sounds of a brief scuffle. Several left. At least two remained.

"Should we check the stairs?"

Silence. The two in hiding readied for the fight.

"Nah. Let's go."

Throughout the early evening patrols walked the alley. They talked as they approached, but when they came to the corner at the bottom of the stairs, their conversations always stopped. They continued in silence.

The two remained in hiding for the long hours. Training and discipline allowed them to remain awake, still and quiet. Sometime after midnight, when they had not heard a patrol for more than an hour, Picaro spoke softly, "In a few hours we will be able to leave."

"Yea."

"Are you alright, Samuel?"

"I've just been thinking."

"About the baby?"

"Yea."

"Me too. In all my life, Samuel, I have never had to see anything like that. My mind will never forget the image of that baby on the steps. So soft, so quiet, so still, so very, very wrong. I remember when my youngest brother was the size of that baby."

"All night we've heard enemy patrols go by. They stopped speaking because of that baby. They didn't come up the stairs because of that baby. Do you know the only reason we're alive right now is because that baby is posted on the steps below? A little baby standing guard for us; a silent word pleading for us; an innocent infant keeping the Forces of the Dark One away from us; a hushed promise protecting us?"

Picaro asked, "Do you think that the woman had to watch her baby die?"

"I don't know. If she did, it must have been a mother's worst nightmare. I think she must have hated you and me for what we did to her baby."

"Us?"

Samuel answered, "Yes, all of us. We choose to be warriors and as a result, a mother's baby dies. You and I play the game of war and an infant must pay the price in order to keep us from dying at the hands of the enemy."

Picaro thought for a few moments and said, "What was the whole purpose of that baby being conceived, born and living for six months? Are we the reason? We should be dead on the street below, not that infant. Was the reason for that baby's existence to die so that we might live?"

Samuel confessed, "I don't know. Surely the woman loved her baby. There was a purpose for that infant's life. There may be a father and grandparents who took great joy from the smiling baby who cooed at them."

"Perhaps an older brother, too, a baby who made others giggle. Was that the purpose for that little one's life?"

"But these address the *why of life*. Picaro, you have really asked about the *why of death*. I don't think you and I are able to answer the *why of death*. However, I do know this; that is what we are left with."

With tears in his eyes, Picaro continued, "Then we must make the baby's death worth more."

"Yes, but how is that done? By killing more?"

"I don't know. But this I do know, slaying in the memory of the nameless infant is hardly good, right and honorable."

The two warriors sat in the hiding place until the dawn fighting began. An hour later they heard the noises of battle in the distance and knew that the Side of the Sun prevailed in the teeter-totter warfare.

Samuel drew a deep breath and stood. After stretching and working the circulation into his legs and backside, he spoke in a tone that Picaro had not heard before.

"My friend, I'm not certain I'll be able to kill again."

Picaro did not answer.

For the first time in all the times before going out to battle, they made no plans. They discussed no strategy. They considered no scenarios. They went downstairs. The baby's body was gone. The body of the woman remained on the steps. Her heart was pierced and broken, her hand stilled and outstretched. It looked as if she had been reaching for and beckoning the baby who was no longer with her, as if she had released and sent forth the infant savior.

CHAPTER 13

THE FINAL BLOW

The war moved to the populated regions to the northeast. The large, seacoast city of Jetty Port became the site of several battles. The Battle of Fish Market and the Three Street Battle were fought in the lower parts of the city while the eight day Battle of Horse Neck Hill devastated the upper district. The awful, excessive loss of life, especially civilian, shocked and ultimately embarrassed the strategists at the war college.

The two warriors, particularly Samuel, no longer possessed the desire to fight. Their mental sharpness disappeared. They conducted planning sessions but did so from habit. Once in the field and underway, they neglected the mission. Their objectives became not to kill and not to be killed; to remain alive and to avoid contact with the enemy.

Late one summer afternoon, Picaro and Samuel made their retreat run during the dusk fight. They looked for ways to elude the enemy and locate places to hide and wait for the advent of the rising orb. They conducted their retreat runs hundreds of times in the previous years, but lately, since the encounter on the stairway, they lost their mental focus.

The two ran through a section of the city with many homes. They avoided the main roadways and the open areas. Back alleys and little used paths provided safe travel. Though they discovered and mentally mapped their escape routes during the day, they became careless and had not taken the extra step in verifying the routes. While making the retreat run during the summer dusk, they became confused about a certain turn. With the enemy closing the distance behind them, Picaro and Samuel paused before choosing the wrong way. The alley they selected quickly ended at the side of a large barn. There was no way through. Instantly they retraced their steps, running furiously in the direction of the enemy. Samuel darted to the left and Picaro followed him. They ran alongside the left bank of a small creek. Hope for escape rose within them as the remote area seemed to move them away from the city. They approached a footbridge and planned to pass under the abutment and continue following the creek to the edge of the city, doing so without discussion. They knew the warriors from the Side of the Sun would reassemble outside the city and they sought their escape to that site.

Samuel focused on their escape, running in full stride and preceding Picaro to safety. Ahead of them a warrior of the Dark One hid under the bridge and watched Samuel approach his position. The enemy considered the ease of this one kill and did not see Picaro who followed twenty-feet behind Samuel. The lead runner approached the hidden man's killing zone and Samuel never saw the ambush. As he darted under the footbridge, the enemy warrior stepped from the shadows and struck Samuel with a mortal blow. Samuel dropped to the ground with a primal grunt. Reacting instantly, Picaro retaliated with equally devastating force. The blow came from the enemy's right side and he slumped to the earth, taking short, irregular, gasping breathes. Both the Dark One's warrior and Picaro's friend were dying on the cursed, blood-soaked earth; the former writhing, the latter physically still as he moaned.

True, Picaro had killed before, but such fighting was generic and business-like. He killed faceless, un-named enemy warriors who fought among and as the Forces of the Dark One. As far as Picaro thought about them and concerned himself with them, they were units. They certainly were not human beings like Samuel or the woman or that baby.

In full rage, Picaro grasped the fallen enemy by the throat. His rigid, sweating fingers closed upon the man's windpipe. He stopped and said, "No, I will not slay you. You will be slain by my friend. Stay alive until I bring him here and he looks you in the eye. That is his right."

After Picaro gagged the dying enemy warrior to quiet him and prevent a call for help, he went to aid his friend. In the shadows of the footbridge, Picaro lifted Samuel to a sitting position and held him. Samuel shook uncontrollably and breathed irregularly. He coughed, groaned and choked. At that moment, Picaro knew Samuel to be incapable of revenge.

"Picaro, I can't see," he gasped while reaching out a hand to the darkness.

"It's night. But I'm here. You can hear me, can't you?"

Samuel, friend to the end, spoke with urgency and concern, "Yes, ... I hear, ... but ... I am dying. ... Run."

"I will not leave you."

Samuel spoke, "Go, for I am not alone. ... He pursued me, has caught me ... and is now drawing near. ... I hear his footfalls."

Picaro jerked his head around and listened to locate the intruder. When convinced no enemy approached, he reassured his friend, "No, it's okay. We are alone. I will not leave you."

Samuel replied, "He's coming after me ... he'll take me."

Thinking that Samuel spoke of the wounded enemy warrior, Picaro attempted to reassure his friend, "Do not be concerned about him. He's not going anywhere. He'll be dead within the hour. He will hurt you no more."

Samuel struggled to a seated position and spoke to one unseen, "Here I am, ... for you called me!"

Picaro tried to calm his delirious friend, "I did not call. Lie down."

Again Samuel arose and spoke, "Here I am."

Picaro said calmly, "I know, I know."

Samuel turned and focused his eyes upon Picaro and announced in short gasps, "Not you. ... Not the enemy. .. Another. He has come for me. ... He's near."

"Who is near?"

"He draws near."

"Who, Samuel? Who is near?"

"Benel."

"Benel? Who's Benel?"

"Benel, the One with Crushed Heel, who walks and runs once more and forever. ... He is here. ... He wants both of us. Picaro, ... he will come after you later."

Samuel turned to speak elsewhere, "Look! ... You want me now and call me by my name. ... Oh yes, I hear the echo. ... I am Samuel. ... Here I am."

Relaxing and sighing, he turned to his friend and confessed, "No more pain, PICARO. Picaro. Picaro."

His named echoed thrice from the dying man's lips, each time half as quiet as before. From his mouth came a final, "Benel."

The last word, spoken softly, accompanied the terminal breath expelled from his lungs. Thus Samuel, the cattle rancher from the High Plains and in recent years warrior for the Side of the Sun, died in the arms of his friend.

Picaro the warrior gnashed his teeth at the loss. After a few moments, he let Samuel's body rest on the ground. With instant, focused rage, he directed his attention to the dying, enemy warrior. The man struggled for each breath. A seething, loathing, foaming hatred welled from deep within Picaro's heart. Their eyes met.

Picaro declared, "You ... I want you to know that you will be the last man I kill."

He slowly prepared his weapon. The gagged warrior grunted. Picaro, perceiving that the dying man wanted to say something, removed the gag.

"Into thy paws, O Benel the Hound, do I commend myself. Thy will be done."

Picaro gasped out loud, "Benel the Hound! What are you talking about?"

The warrior gasped and replied, "The Hunter's hound. ... You heard your friend speak of him. ... Benel, the One with Crushed Heel, ... Who walks and runs once more and forever. ... The blessed wind has given him your scent. ... The Hunter is after you. ... He has sent the hound to track you down, ... just as he did with your friend and ... just as he did with me."

"Your life is over."

"What is your friend's name?"

Picaro spit venom back, "Shut your mouth. Your filthy lips will never speak the word of his name. As I said, your life is over."

"Good. ... You kill me and Benel the Hound will retrieve me to the Hunter. ... Your friend and I will be with each other shortly. ... In a moment we will see each other and rejoice. ... We'll be together forever. ... The Hunter, the Hound, the Blessed Wind, your friend and me. ... My life will just be starting."

"Then let it begin now!"

As horrible as it may seem, Picaro struck the man with a blow intending to kill not only the warrior, but also the Hunter and his hound. In the deathly stillness of that evening, Picaro heard only his own breathing. Then somewhere in the darkness, either upstream or down, a hound bayed thrice.

CHAPTER 14

THE PROCLAMATION

Picaro removed the uniform from the fallen, enemy warrior and hid the body behind a shrub hedge near the end of the footbridge. A warrior's body without a uniform would arouse suspicion in both camps and word about a spy might even be sent to the war strategists. Picaro had no time to care for Samuel's body. He knew that the midnight patrol would dispose of it with all the honor due a fallen warrior.

Voices downstream indicated the enemy approached. Picaro hurried to change into the uniform of the Forces of the Dark One. He turned his face to the sound and saw several warriors. Had he not been in the shadows of the footbridge they would have seen him as well. Picaro rolled up his old uniform and placed it in his dirty pack. Thirty feet separated him from the advancing patrol, giving him enough time to take the enemy warrior's weapon and shout in a commanding voice of authority, "Halt!"

The three warriors reacted by stopping, training their weapons and readying for a fight.

Picaro continued, "Lower your weapons and continue your patrol."

One replied, "Step out of the shadows."

Picaro did. When the others saw he wore the uniform of their side, they lowered their weapons and relaxed."

The same one asked, "Why did you tell us to halt?"

Picaro answered, "Think about it. If you kept coming without me giving you a warning that I was here, you would have met me in the dark shadows. You might have been so startled you would have done something stupid. I might have hurt you by defending myself."

A young voice replied with a tone of confidence, "Or you might have been severely injured by me. You are older than the average warrior. You better be more careful. How long you been at war, old man?"

Picaro spoke with disdain and rancor, "Long enough to do away with better warriors than you. If I had been a member of the other side, you'd be dead right now."

The young voice continued, "Really? You threaten very well, but all I hear is talk from you."

"That's because you don't pay enough attention to what is around you."

Picaro motioned to the body of Samuel and said, "You don't hear any talk from him, do you? As I said, if I were a member of the other side, your mother would soon be receiving a regret letter."

Silence heightened the threats for a moment. The one who spoke first, spoke again, "Alright, let's continue our patrol."

Picaro experienced conflicting emotions, grief at Samuel's death met relief at his own escape. He felt guilty over having to use Samuel's body to escape while the feelings of pride as he commended himself for such quick thinking repulsed him and greater guilt waved over him at having to leave the body of his friend for someone else to find. He vacillated with anxious fear and undirected anger, with crushing sorrow and awful wretchedness, with unmoving regret and wrenching despair. But the consuming guilt always waited to engulf him further and deeper, like an ocean of yellow goo weighing him down and drawing him to its bottomless pit. In the nights that followed, Picaro thought that he had killed Samuel. He pledged to himself and to no other, that he would kill no more and proclaimed it to the vaulted canopy and shadowy sky above him, "No more!"

For the next five months, Picaro wore the uniform of the Forces of the Dark One at night and the uniform of the Side of the Sun at day. He remained near the battle line at all times. At dawn and at dusk, when the line moved forward or backward, Picaro changed his uniform. Since he perceived no differences between the sides and sought to fight no more, Picaro confessed no creed and pledged no allegiance. He had to look at his sleeve to know which side he served. He knew that he no longer belonged.

The days and nights defined themselves, but the weeks and months and towns and cities blended into a continuous blur. At a battle in the country, or was it in the city, Picaro decided his only escape from the warrior's life was to "fulfill the sevens." Having fought the seven types of warfare and battled in the seven terrain campaigns, he immediately met two of the three sevens. Of the seven years, less than a year remained.

Picaro had no will left to be a warrior. The cities provided many places of refuge for hiding. The attics above the dens of strong drink served as excellent hiding places. Warriors tended not to destroy those establishments. Picaro entered the den and located the attic entrance. Later, during the liveliest part of the late night, he made his way to the hiding place. He became as adept at hiding as he had been at staying alive in battle. Staying in the dens made him remember the times when his mother and he stood outside the den of strong drink waiting for Mac. He loathed both those days back then and the nights in the attics now.

That spring the rains consumed the land and left it soggy. While the torrents of rain ceased, the prolonged drizzle did not. Fog filled both unlit streets and weak lungs. Mist immersed alleys and permeated his clothing. The dampness crept into his tired, weary bones. Picaro, aged more by experiences than years, felt the wet cold invade his body and touch his back. When the mist penetrated deep into his lungs, he began to cough and feel heavy. His temperature rose and he knew he needed to find a place to stay for more than the night. Spasms of uncontrollable shivering and disorientation commenced as the fever increased. He abandoned his weapon somewhere and did not care. His mental sharpness deteriorated and along with it, the usual caution and care for himself. He had to find a place to stay quickly or he would pass out in the street. All doors remained shut to him and the buildings cast no light. One thought drove him -- get to the outside of town and find a barn or shed or stable. Coughing and grimacing as he held his painful chest, he ran. After a heavy blink, his heavy eyes focused on a building ahead of him. This had to be the place where he would hide. He was capable of going no farther. Like the other buildings, this one remained dark and locked. Picaro tried a side window and slid it open. He hoisted himself to the sill, forced himself through the window and tumbled to the floor. A set of stairs ascended to the right and instinctively he climbed them, being able to do so only on hands and knees. After crawling as far as he could will himself into the upper room, he lost consciousness.

There he slept until a single, piercing voice sounded and echoed. The words wormed into his groggy mind as if spoken from a great distance in a dream, "In the Name of the Hunter and the Hound and the Blessed Wind." A massive "Ah yes," sung by many, filled the air.

Picaro's face, head and shoulder ached to his bones. He grimaced as he rolled to his back and clamped his free hand over his mouth to prevent a moan from becoming audible and revealing his presence. His arm, shoulder and face tingled as the blood slowly returned to these pained, anemic places. Picaro's awareness of himself intensified and faded. When Picaro woke completely, he heard the collective voice speak again.

"I believe in the Hunter, the majestic Maker and Owner of all seen and unseen. And I believe in Benel his only Hound our Master, who was sent by the Hunter, suffered under the principalities and powers, was entrapped by the heel, crushed and bled to death. In victory, he howled at the moon and the fallen stars. In triumph, he bayed in the dark and deep places. On the third day he broke the iron jaws of the death trap, and now, with

Crushed Heel, the Blood Hound walks and runs once more and forever. I believe in the Blessed Wind who sustains the many and who blows where he wills carrying scents to the Blood Hound who pursues until the last of time. Ah yes."

Picaro now understood what happened to him and where he now was. In his delirious state two nights earlier, he wandered into the upstairs balcony of a holy place. Evidently his fever broke in the late night or early morning and he slept quietly until the assembly of the Hunter's captives began. The pains in his shoulder and face eased, being replaced by intense thirst and hunger pangs. However, according to the self-discipline practiced for years, he remained quiet and in place lest he be discovered.

A single voice, speaking from below, echoed off the vaulted ceiling above, "Dear fellow pursued, caught and kept of the Great Blood Hound, the proclamation for this day is based upon the Sacred Word written by the holy scribe. Please listen to the reading as we consider the truth this morning that *The War Is Over and Peace Reigns.*"

Having no option, Picaro listened intently. Besides, the theme intrigued him, the man who resolved to fight no more.

The voice continued with the reading, "'Console, console my beloved,' speaks the Only One. 'Breathe into my beloved's ear and whisper to her that her warfare is over. Let her know that she has received from me twice what she deserves for her sins.'"

What a consolation thought Picaro. Let this woman know that she will be loved and cared for when she has received a double beating for all her wrongs. Picaro knew the wife of a man at the sawmill who had been beaten many times by her husband. Picaro recalled her shamed look when seen by others. She stayed inside her shack and when she had to leave it, she walked about the camp with her eyes to the ground. The woman cowered as if she had somehow actually deserved her bruises and blackened eyes. The words spoken by the guardian of the holy place sickened Picaro as he remembered how he hated and loathed that brutal man for the senseless beatings he gave his wife and for having caused her so much pain and sorrow.

The voice continued, "As you are fully aware, the war has moved into our city. The governing authorities have named it the Battle of Two Buckets. While most civilians have been able to avoid being hurt, several buildings and homes of members have been damaged. The fighting has lasted for two days now and it should be over in four or five days. The Forces of the Dark One and the Side of the Sun will leave our city. The bloodshed and destruction will cease and we will be left to clean up and rebuild. We look forward to that time and will certainly want to help our neighbors in whatever ways we can, especially those belonging to the Hunter."

The hidden one in the holy place listened and pondered these things.

"The battle in our city reminds us of the warfare declared by the Hunter. Only in that conflict we were neither guiltless spectators nor innocent victims. The battle line was drawn. All humanity stood on one side and the Only One on the other. All we like deserters slouched on the other side of the battlefield and took up our natural positions against the Hunter, the Hound and the Blessed Wind. As faithless warriors we camped with the allies of the Fallen One and volunteered to be enemies of the Only One."

The lapsed warrior in the loft hated the Hunter. Had he not been hiding, and therefore trapped in the holy place, he would have fled to the battlefield and to the world outside.

"Our violations against the Only One were not only done in deeds and spoken in words. The Only One, who knows all things, is aware of our very thoughts. What to do with such traitorous people? What to do? The full payment must be made; a complete penalty must be exacted. So the Hunter sent his only hound, Benel the Blood Hound, into this fallen world. He ..."

Picaro hardly contained himself as he thought of this action and muttered to himself, "The great hunter is not willing to do his own dirty work. He sends out his hound to track, pursue, run down and catch the supposed culprits. Then this mighty hunter comes sauntering up to claim the prey. The helpless victim is mercilessly subjected to a double-beating. Oh what glory! With every fiber of my being, I will fight that blood hound. If he catches me, I will resist him to the end."

"... and do you not see Benel allow them to take him captive. The animal makes no sound, even when they cut him in the administration of the *Thirteen Knives Used Thrice*. He endures that for you, for me and for all people. They condemn the hound to slow death. Benel permits them to drag him to the *Place of the Snare* and there they hold his back leg steady while pressing the trigger pan from the underside. The steel-jaw trap is released crushing his heel. The trap has sharp teeth which bite and hold Benel's leg in place. But behold, the animal did not attempt to free himself. He did not test the chain attached to the trap and pegged to the ground. The mighty and powerful hound stayed in place with holy blood flowing from his crushing wound. There, dear people, yes, there is where the double payment was made, a completed price. What we owed was paid twice. When the sacrifice was sufficient, doubly sufficient, Benel the Blood Hound, with the last bit of energy he could summon, lifted his snout and gave a deep, long bay that has echoed down through the centuries. Then he died. His breath left him and by his ..."

The man hidden in the upstairs of the holy place smirked and snarled to himself, "Benel the Stupid. The hound got exactly what he deserved, letting himself be taken captive like that. How in the world is that supposed to help anyone? How do these people believe such rubbish?"

For a few moments, he pondered all these things.

"... death could not hold him. Benel, the One with Crushed Heel, walks and runs once more and forever. Ah yes."

"Ah yes," echoed the people.

Picaro heard the baying of a hound. He thought it had been staged by the guardian as a dramatic closure to his proclamation for the day. Picaro erred. The sound came from Benel the Blood Hound and at that moment only Picaro heard it.

"The undeserved riches of our Hound Benel, the love of the Hunter and the continued abiding of the Blessed Wind be with you all."

"Ah yes."

The hound bayed again. Picaro erred once more.

CHAPTER 15

TWO CONVERSATIONS

The divine service concluded with the whisper-singing of a hymn. The hidden warrior could not make out the words, but the refrain became distinct, "All glory to the One Who is Three, yes praise and honor alone to Thee." After the hymn, the people remained in their places until directed to leave. Music ascended in the room from the recorder quartet with the wooden bass recorder providing a particularly haunting echo. The worshipers spoke in subdued conversation and as the people slowly departed, the room gradually became quieter.

Picaro, who observed none of this because of his location, listened to the words within the holy place. He heard snippets of conversations, "... was right about the work being done ... but no battle damage on the other side of the roadway ... probably, but you can't make him believe ... see ya, the Only One be with you, Mo ... and also with you."

"Guardian, may I speak with you for a few minutes. When would you have some time?"

The overseer of the holy place answered the woman, "Now is fine. Is this place alright?"

"Yes."

"Please, let's sit down here."

The woman and the guardian had been near the door at the back of the room and after moving to a bench sat directly below Picaro. Thus, the stranger in the balcony heard every word spoken between the guardian and the woman.

"Guardian, I am from another city and I belong to a holy place where many of the Other Ones are worshiped. Because of this horrible situation, I am not able to speak to the overseer there. I hold that there are no others but the Only One. The overseer there does not believe as I do. From this morning's service and from your proclamation here, I think that you believe as I do. Or rather, I believe as you do. Am I correct?"

"I believe, teach and confess that there is only the One. He is Hunter and Hound and Wind. I unconditionally subscribe to the creed we confessed today. It declares what I believe, or as you say, I believe what it declares."

"That makes me feel much better."

"Fine. Ma'am, it is not necessary for me to know the name of your city, your holy place or your overseer, but may I know your name?"

"I'm sorry. I'm called Vivian the Timid."

"May I call you Vivian?"

"You may call me either. I'm not offended by being addressed as Vivian the Timid. The name describes me adequately. But let me not waste any more of your time. Guardian, for nearly three months I have been trying to come here to speak with you."

"What prevented you from doing so?"

She chuckled seriously and sighed, "Me."

Unbeknownst to Picaro, the guardian smiled. The woman saw him smile and smiled herself.

"Well, Vivian the Timid, what made you finally come here must be quite serious."

"It is. It's my son. He's 28 years old and I worry about him. He dwells with a woman who is not his wife. My son knows this is not the will and way of the Hunter. But the pull of the woman is stronger now than the conviction of his heart and the way of his belief. She is leading him to Sophia and I fear for what might happen to him. My daily supplications ascend to the place of the Hunter. The son of my sorrow makes me weep each night. He is, and his name is, Benoni."

"Has he always been Benoni?"

"Yes, but it was not his fault. A week before he was born my husband died. I have been a widow since that day and Benoni is my only child."

"You said your son knows the word and will of the Hunter?"

"Yes. My Benoni heard the *Thrice Calling of the Echo* when he was eight days old. The accounts and deeds of the Hunter and the Hound have been told to my son from the earliest of his days. He is well acquainted with them. He has heard the great hymns from before he drew his first breath as I sang them to him when he was an unborn child in my womb. I whisper-spoke them to him in his cradle. At age three he began to tell them back to me. So yes, guardian, Benoni knows the will, promises, word and holy blessings of the Hunter."

"Vivian the Timid, do you honestly believe that the Hunter, having once held your son, will let him go so easily? The word of the proclamation has been carried by the Wind and even now the Hound is pursuing Benoni. The Hunter had your son and wants him back. He who did not spare his own Hound once will send him out again. Relentless is Benel's pursuit. He is determined and tireless. Your son will not be at peace with himself until he turns and returns. Does your son live near you?"

"No, he lives farther south, far from my reach. I know there is not much I can do, but I needed to talk to someone. Guardian, will you please remember my son in your personal supplications?"

"Yes, both you and your son. May we do so right now?"

"Please."

"Dear loving and heavenly Hunter, as you know, the heart of Vivian the Timid hurts for her son. She wants only what you want for him. Please continue to send forth your Hound to track him down. O dear One, pursue Benoni until he is turned and is returned. If it be necessary, make his life miserable until he cries out for the peace that he once had. We petition you also on behalf of the woman who is with Benoni. Pursue her as well and grant that she be enlightened through the proclamation given to Benoni. Still the quiet spirit of Vivian the Timid and give her peace. Continue to receive her and the many supplications she places before you. Grant her safe journey to her home. May your good and gracious will be done, O Hunter, in the Name of the Hound. Ah yes."

"Ah yes," echoed Vivian the Timid.

The overseer spoke again, "You do understand that this supplication may be answered tomorrow, or it may take a long time? When you put such matters into his care, the timing is according to him as well. He may require longsuffering and great patience of you, Vivian the Timid. It might be that his work with Benoni may not be accomplished during your lifetime."

"Yes, I know that, guardian. I even understand that the Hunter may have to use the occasion of my death as the event leading my son back to him."

"Woman, you must consider changing your name. I suggest Vivian the Wise."

She deflected his suggestion, "I must go now. Thank you, guardian. I will remember you in my personal supplications. I will ask him to keep you faithful in your belief, steadfast in your confession and strong as you lead the people in the divine service. Announce the proclamation and proclaim the announcements of the Only One."

"Thank you. May the Only One be with you."

"And also with you."

Picaro heard the door to the outside close. There were no sounds inside the holy place. Again, and even more so, he felt he had violated a sanctified law despite his undesired intrusion on the private conversation. His unintentional eavesdropping not only made him tense, but also guilt-laden, as if his presence had desecrated a holy event. Being forced to listen to their conversation made him uncomfortable. Hearing the guardian's supplication to the Hunter on behalf of the woman with petitions for the hound to pursue her son, pierced the warrior's soul with anguish. He closed his eyes and thought about his situation. Because he relaxed, Picaro neither heard nor saw the guardian ascend the stairs and walk to where he was. The warrior did not know of the guardian's presence until the latter spoke.

"I see you are much better."

Instinctively, Picaro grabbed for his weapon and jerked to a crouched position. Though the grab was fruitless, the defensive posture enabled Picaro to spring in attack. In an instant, the robed guardian lay on his back and Picaro's left hand squeezed the overseer's throat. The metal plate carried by the overseer now twirled on the floor beside him.

The guardian gurgled, "If your weapon is nearby, I promise not to move until you get it and return."

Picaro realized how ridiculous he must have looked to the guardian. He felt stupid and noted how awkward he was in this holy place and how everything he thought and did in the place seemed wrong.

"I'm sorry. I didn't hear you come up the stairs. You startled me."

The ruffled guardian was mildly surprised, "Really? Uh, what I mean is, I didn't want to disturb you if you were still sleeping."

Picaro understood what he meant and replied in a tone of slight resignation, "I'm not much of a warrior, am I? You have humiliated me."

"I didn't intend to do so," the guardian replied, "I only wanted to bring a plate of food to you. If I found you asleep I planned to leave it. When you woke, it would be here and ready for you. It's not much, but I thought you might be hungry."

The overseer retrieved the metal plate and began to gather the scattered food. Picaro started to help but stopped when he found a card.

> *I am Roland the Officiant from the*
> *ancient village of Benedicamus*
> *at the base of High Mountain.*
> *I may speak to you.*
>
> *(Please keep this card.)*

Picaro spoke slowly as if in continuous thought, "Years ago I saw cards similar to this one. I forgot about them. I was only a kid at the time. About ten years ago cards like these were given to me. They were different somehow. Oh yea, I remember. The other cards indicated that the card holders did not have permission to speak to me. Yes, and uh, right, ... I had to return the card."

Roland the Officiant frowned, "Where did this happen?"

"A long way from here. It is in the deep woods to the north and west of this land. A month of steady walking might be enough to get there. Why do you ask?"

"I have heard of such persecutions and I often remember my brothers who have been silenced from the proclamation. Do you remember their names?"

Picaro answered immediately, "No, not at all. It all seemed quite silly to me at the time. Anyway, had the tongues of those men been removed?"

"What?"

"Their cards indicated that they could not speak to me. Now you tell me they had been silenced. What was done to them?"

The guardian gave a stifled laugh and explained, "There was nothing physically done to them. Citizens passed local laws preventing them from doing what I do here. Now all of us are required to carry these cards. The cards indicate if we are permitted or not. I am permitted here, but I have to be careful. Spies are everywhere, even here this morning. They look and listen for something to use against me. They want to force me to bring in other ones to worship. They know if they can force me to do so, I will resign as guardian."

Picaro replied in a somewhat uninterested tone, "Sounds rather political to me." He picked up the other card from the floor and read it.

```
"No liturgy" is heard from their throats,
"We want to sing 'Sow Your Wild Oats'."
    So they follow the craze,
    Put the sheep out to graze,
And instead they entertain goats.
```

Picaro asked, "What is this all about?"

The guardian replied, "Understanding that may have to wait until another day. I believe what is really important for you right now is printed on the other side."

Picaro turned the card over and read the other side.

```
        The Hunter is after you.
The Wind has given your scent
            to His Hound.
        At this very moment
    His Hound is tracking you.
```

Picaro stiffened within. He attempted to hide his resistance from the guardian though he immediately knew his attempt failed. Picaro attempted to take the offensive, "And why, Roland the Officiant, why would you think that this side of the card is especially important for me today?"

The guardian gave a feigned look of confusion and answered, "Well, you said that a decade ago what was written on the card seemed quite silly. You gave the distinct impression that it no longer is so frivolous. Am I wrong?"

Picaro took the food from the plate and put it in the large pocket of his jacket. He stood to leave. The guardian did not move out of the way, but remained kneeling as he continued to pick up the crumbs.

"Yes, you are wrong. I must be leaving now."

The guardian replied in a non-threatening but firm voice, "No, my friend, you should not be leaving now."

Picaro stiffened and challenged, "And why not?"

The guardian attempted to shift his attention, "May I ask your name?"

"You may ask. I won't answer. Why shouldn't I leave, guardian?"

"Because it is midday and you have on the uniform of the Forces of the Dark One."

The warrior sighed in self-disgust.

Roland the Officiant spoke in a calm voice, "You are safe here and may stay until the night comes."

"Thank you."

"You're welcome. Oh, by the way, the Hound pursues you. He is quite near to you and, even if I don't, he knows your name."

Picaro snapped back, "Look, simply because I have been subjected to a silly *Thrice Calling* ceremony, doesn't mean that I have obligated myself to anything!"

"Indeed not, my friend. Rather, it means the Hunter is obligated. Anyway, I didn't know that you had been thrice called. I meant merely that by hearing the proclamation this morning, the Hound knows your name and is pursuing you. It matters not. Whether by the thrice calling or the hearing of the proclamation, at that instant it occurred. The Hound began his pursuit of you, doing so long before the creation of time."

"Nothing of what you say makes any sense."

"Do you have to understand something before it is true?"

"Look, I release the hound from his obligation."

The guardian chuckled to himself and continued, "It's not so easy."

Picaro replied quickly, "I did not have very much difficulty in saying it, did I?"

"Please, you misunderstand me. It is not so easy for the Hound to be released from his obligation. He is like a loving parent whose child has gone astray. I think you heard the proclamation this day. Or am I wrong?"

"No, guardian, you are not wrong."

"Then you probably also heard my conversation with the woman?"

"Yes," he confessed and then added in a different tone, "but I had no choice. I'm quite sorry. I didn't want to hear a single word of it."

"No matter. Perhaps the Hunter wanted you to hear it. He pursues in strange ways, you know. Incidentally, Vivian the Timid is not your mother, is she?"

"No."

Roland the Officiant added, "Is your mother still living?"

Picaro felt the increased pressure and the consuming guilt. He fended off the attack by saying, "I haven't spoken with her in the last few days."

"Just thought I'd ask. I will leave you now. The Only One be with you."

Later, Picaro wondered if it was the holy place, or the timing of the guardian, or the remembering of the divine service that almost made him say, "And also with you"?

Instead he responded with a clumsy, "And also good-bye to you. Uhh, I thank you for the food and shelter."

The guardian left. Picaro ate the bread, the cheese and one of the two apples. He changed into the uniform of the Side of the Sun and waited a half hour before leaving by the back door. He jogged along the wooded path. Fifty feet from the holy place Roland the Officiant sat on a bench off the path. Without looking at Picaro, the guardian said, "Do you hear what I heard?"

CHAPTER 16

WATCHER AND WATCHED

Months passed and Picaro fulfilled the sevens during the Battle of Rhubarb Ridge. He reported to the leaders of the Side of the Sun and informed them that he had completed his time as a warrior in view of his fulfilling the sevens. Since only three warriors ever accomplished this feat, the leaders planned to have a special ceremony. But Picaro, after dressing in civilian clothes, left without acknowledgment or decoration.

Delighting in full feeling of liberation, Picaro traveled in the general direction of The Dell, that is, to the north and west. The binding of his uniforms no longer held him and he felt a return to the days of his youth. But the war had made him age beyond his years. No longer was he the young, carefree stag bounding through the forest. Picaro, now the battle-scarred mountain lion with keen eyes, scanned the landscape and made strategy assessments.

The war consumed a large part of his life and with it now over for him, the veteran soon discovered a deep vacuum within. The ever-deepening hole, caused by undefined guilt and unfulfilled purpose, abscessed within and gnawed at him. He missed something and ached for a life he could not describe. A longing need peered out from him seeking to draw something or someone in.

Dear little ones, had Picaro thought about it at length, he would have remembered this same aching as a little boy. When his mother took him and his brothers away, an empty spot remained where his father had been. Children and young adults who suffer the death of mother or father, or whose parents divorce know this undefined feeling. These are sinister, empty hurts that many young people don't want to talk about, nor should they be forced. Nevertheless, they do think about these matters.

During the next six months, Picaro's journey reflected his vacant life. Except for the time necessary to purchase supplies, he avoided the cities and towns. He did various jobs, working only long enough to earn and convert food money. At night, he remained in the woods where he slept the light sleep of a restless soul. He did not build fires because they might attract attention. He borrowed sheds and barns on rainy nights and left before dawn. His travels varied, but they always tended to the north and west. This put him on the high plains where the wind blew, though there were no evergreens to play the soft, needled music in the breezes of the evening.

One warm, summer night, after the wind stilled, Picaro sat leaning his back against a large oak tree. There were other trees in the large, wooded area, mostly willow and a few maple. With the dirt road forty feet from him, Picaro settled into a hidden spot where he could view the road for a hundred feet in both directions. He sat among the dark shadows of the trees and watched. The full moon illuminated the road and the fields beyond. It also provided him protection in the dark place.

Shortly before midnight someone approached on the road and Picaro heard the footfall of the night traveler. Before he saw the person, he understood from the sounds that the traveler ran alone, carried no great burden, had been running for some time and had long legs. Though he made no movement, the veteran tensed as the runner drew near. The panoramic view allowed Picaro to watch the intruder for fifteen to twenty seconds. The older boy neither looked to the side nor slowed his pace. In a few seconds, the darkness of the night swallowed him.

According to habit, Picaro waited a few minutes and moved several hundred feet to a new sleeping spot, one deeper into the woods. There he sat thinking about the incident. As he ran by, the boy had no idea that someone watched him from the shadows. Whether the watcher meant him harm or not, the boy was being watched. Picaro continued thinking. Like the days of his youth, Picaro may have been watched by someone as he raced home from the sawmill at night. Mostly, he feared the Other who inhabited the dark places. As a young man, he feared the Other who lurked about the shadows. But now Picaro had visited the shadows, taken up residence within them and found himself alone amidst the shades of the night. The victory over his fears was a battle waged against the One called the Other. The Other had not only been defeated but also supplanted. To that boy who had just jogged by, Picaro was now the Other - the Incarnate Other.

There were two worlds now, two realities. The runner was a part of the first world and knew nothing about Picaro's existence in the second. Picaro reasoned that those of the second world were aware of the first world and had certain advantages and exercised controls over those within it. He might elect to act or choose to neglect. He could act for a specific purpose or on a whim. He knew that had he wanted to, he could have slain the boy without him ever seeing Picaro or knowing his name. The Incarnate Other in the hidden world might seek to help but that would require knowledge, desire and compassion. But how would the boy perceive such a visit? If he knew Picaro lurked in the darkness, the boy would be terrified and run farther and faster to get away from him, even if Picaro only wanted to help.

An awful thought entered his mind and a chill enveloped him as he considered this. There might be a third world beyond his, another reality beyond the shadows, one much deeper and more hidden. From within that dimension, One might now be watching Picaro sit under a lonely tree in a land of dark shadows. Picaro shuddered at his next thought. If such a reality existed, then Picaro became the runner once again. While the Other no longer chased him, some other One now pursued him. Pursuing! Picaro knew that, had the other One so desired, *It* could slay him at any instant.

With venomed tongue, he whisper-spoke into that dark abyss, "Hunter, I hate you and the hound whom you have sent. I will kill him if I am able."

An hour later, Picaro dozed and while he slept a gusty breeze rushed through the broad leaves of the maple trees. A baying sounded through the tops of the trees. Picaro woke in an instant. He listened intently. The gust ceased, now replaced by a gentle breeze within the woods. The baying ceased, now replaced by a haunting echo within the runner.

"PICARO ... **Picaro** ... picaro."

His head dismissed it as part of a dream. His heart doubted his head. His soul knew the truth.

Picaro turned over and muttered before falling asleep, "I will kill you."

The quiet response gently brushed over him, "Picaro, you already have."

CHAPTER 17

SOMEONE'S WAGON IS FIXED

Two months later Picaro approached the town of Water, so named because of need rather than abundance. The morning birds sang their final songs as they prepared to migrate to the southwest. Rays from the sun prepared to flood the fields of corn and soybean. The cold air prophesied the advent of the frost, causing farmers to use every minute of daylight until harvest home.

Ahead of him, at the side of the country road, Picaro approached a wagon loaded high with brush. A lone figure knelt at the side of the wagon, apparently examining the left rear wheel. As Picaro came to the place, the sun rose, splashing the landscape with first rays of copper light. Though his long shadow fell directly below the rear axle, thereby warning the person, Picaro wanted to make certain the wagoner knew of his presence. Since the person wore a cloak and white scarf, he thought the individual to be a woman and consequently, some twenty feet from the wagon, he cleared his throat and spoke in a non-threatening tone.

"Do you need some help?"

The individual turned and stood. As she did, the white scarf fell from her head to her shoulders. The golden rays from the autumn sun deepened the color of her red hair. Faint freckles highlighted her light complexion and set the stage for her sparkling, green eyes. This epiphany stunned Picaro. The woman raised her right arm to fend off the light. Picaro moved to the side, not so much to permit her to lower her arm, but that he might again behold her face without the shadow.

"Yes," she answered.

He mumbled, "Yes, what?"

"Yes, I need some help. This rear wheel seems to be broken. It won't turn and is skidding."

He forced himself to turn his eyes away from her and focus his attention on the wheel. How he willed to be able to fix the wheel, but it had seized and could not be repaired here. He thought of ways to rig it for a short travel.

He looked at the brush piled on the wagon and asked, "This is not a heavy load, is it?"

She replied, "No, only raspberry canes. I am hauling them from the berry field to our yard."

"Is there anything under these canes?"

"A few boards, I think."

He lifted the canes from the underside and saw the boards. One was a long two-by-four and another was a shorter one-by-six. Picaro had an idea and asked, "How far is it to your yard?"

Pointing in the direction she had been going, she answered his question, "Ahead to that small grove of trees. Our house is there; maybe half a mile."

The dirt road remained level until just before the trees, where it rose slightly. He pulled the boards from the raspberry canes and placed the two-by-four under the wagon on the left side. He levered the one-by-six under the rear axle on the left side in order to lift the wagon.

"After I lift this axle and the wheel comes off the ground, you put that end of the two-by-four on top of the front frame. Make sure that the two-by-four is on edge, not flat. We'll need to work together as a team."

"Okay," she said.

Picaro raised the back of the wagon a foot off the ground and said, "Okay." The woman quickly placed the end of the board on the front frame. He lowered the back of the wagon causing the axle to rest on the two-by-four. The left rear wheel no longer touched the ground. In an attempt to reduce the weight on that wheel, he shoved as many of the canes as he could to the right side of the wagon.

"We're ready," he announced. "You sit on the right side and control the reigns from there. I'll walk along this side, checking to make sure that the board doesn't slip off the frame and that the bad wheel doesn't touch the ground."

In an attempt to be with this woman longer, Picaro said, "We'll take this slow. There's no need to hurry. Is that okay with you?"

She relaxed and responded with a sense of relief which Picaro detected as she spoke, "That will be fine. Thank you."

The woman signaled the horse to pull and the wagon moved forward. Immediately the scraping sound of the board was heard as it furrowed a one inch rut in the dirt road. The wheel continued to clear the ground and Picaro continued to steal glances at this captivating young woman.

She noticed and wondered aloud, "Is everything alright?"

"Just fine," he replied, giving an exaggerated inspection of the axle and looking at the long rut caused by the two-by-four.

In a warm and inviting tone she spoke to him, "My name's Roja. I live on a farm with my parents and younger sisters. My father is Herman, but he is known among the people here as Herm the Razzberry Man. He and my mother were born in this area and have lived and farmed here all their lives. Mom loves to cook. She's really the best cook around. The children in the area like to stop by for a treat from the kitchen, especially when they know she's been baking. What's your name?"

"My name is Picaro." He regretted that his answer sounded a bit short and impersonal. "What I mean is, my name is Picaro." That sounded worse and he decided not to make another correction.

"Well, Mr. Picaro, I'm glad you stopped by."

"Please, just Picaro; no mister, okay?"

"Alright, Picaro." She sounded more personal and hearing her say his name was, ... well, it was pleasant.

She continued, "Where is your home, Picaro?"

He thought for a moment, then said, "I was born in the Northwoods far west and north of this place."

"Is that home for you, now?"

Her voice sounded clear and sweet. He had to concentrate on her question in order to answer her.

"Not really. It's probably been ten years or so since I've been there. My mother was there at that time, my two younger brothers as well. Other than that, I am alone."

"Picaro, you seem rather mysterious. Am I asking you questions you'd just as soon not answer? It's really none of my business, you know."

Picaro had not often heard a young woman's voice in his life. He enjoyed listening to her. He replied, "No, uh ... Roja. I guess I am just not used to talking about myself and my past." He added quickly, "But you may ask me whatever you want."

She accepted his invitation, "Well, okay, what have you been doing for ten years away from home?"

"I've been a warrior."

"Which side?"

Picaro took a second before answering. Her question made him feel guilty. But why? She had no idea of his uniform exchanges. He answered, "The Side of the Sun."

"Good," Roja announced and continued. "So, are you heading back home now?"

Again he thought prior to responding. He wondered why her questions caused him such difficulty.

"No, I guess I'm not really heading back home. To be truthful, Roja, I'm not certain that what I remember as home even exists any more. Honestly, my plan consisted of walking this road into town today. That's about as far ahead as I had planned."

"Well then, Picaro, have you made any particular plans for breakfast this morning?"

"No," he replied eagerly, though immediately convinced that his answer didn't sound extremely intelligent.

"Good," she said pertly, "then you may eat with us. Breakfast should be just about ready."

"You and your family haven't eaten yet?"

"No. We all have chores to do before breakfast. I went to the lower raspberry field to load the canes and haul them back to the yard. When the wagon broke down, you came along. Your clever solution permits me to return in time to eat breakfast this morning. So it seems only fair that you join us. Don't you agree, Picaro?"

He replied in a more confident tone, "Yes, that would be fine. I must admit I am hungry."

The horse turned onto the roadway leading to the farmhouse. The two-by-four continued to gouge an unbroken groove. An older man, having heard the scraping sound from afar, slowly walked from a back barn to the house. The farmer stopped at the porch step, glared at his gimpy wagon, stared at the strange man walking beside the wagon and scrutinized the long rut.

As Roja spoke she gave the horse a drink of water, "Good morning, dad. The wagon broke down and this kind man helped me get it back here. Picaro is his name."

Herm the Razzberry man's expression did not change as he uttered a simple, "Hullo."

"Good morning to you, sir," the veteran warrior nervously responded.

Roja interrupted the stilted exchange, "Dad, since he helped us out, I invited him to have breakfast with us. Is that okay?"

He said, "Yup," and went inside the house.

Roja whispered to Picaro, "I think he likes you." Picaro gave a wry grin as she motioned him to follow her into the house.

Throughout the meal, Roja's father neither spoke nor changed expression nor even looked at Picaro. Roja's sisters and their mother conversed, trying to include Picaro. His short responses revealed his frazzled state of mind.

During the farm breakfast, Picaro thought about asking for a few days work. He had asked many others for work or permission to sleep in a shed or barn. Now he experienced trouble knowing when to ask, what to ask and how to ask. While Roja made him slightly anxious, Herm the Razzberry Man unnerved him. Picaro didn't want the others to think him forward, as if he would stay only on her account. Likewise, he enjoyed talking with her and didn't especially want to leave after eating. Roja interceded for him.

"Dad, you know Picaro might be able to help you with all the things that you don't have time to fix around the place. He has no plans requiring him to be anywhere. Maybe he could stay for awhile to help us out with those things we never seem to get around to."

Her dad's expression did not change as he answered, "He's got one hour from this minute to get that wagon wheel working properly. If it's done within the hour then I'll find work for him for several days."

Picaro tensed in his desire to begin working on the wheel. He slid his chair back slightly, intending to rise. At the instant he resolved to stand up and begin, Roja's father announced as he looked at the clock, "The hour has begun. But before our guest begins his work, I believe he would like to drink another cup of coffee."

Picaro wanted, and indeed, started to say "no thank you," but the tone of his elder's voice prevented him, perceiving it more order than invitation.

Herm the Razzberry Man stood up, sauntered to the stove, grabbed a hot pad, took the steaming coffee pot, slowly walked to Picaro, poured him a cup of coffee and filled it to the brim.

Picaro tried to drink his coffee without appearing to be in a hurry. The farmer's expression didn't change. Indeed, after finishing the cup of coffee so quickly, it took a week before the inside of Picaro's mouth healed. With the last swallow gulped and still stinging his mouth, Picaro went to work. As Picaro left the house, Herm the Razzberry Man's expression changed. It began with a pinch of snuff placed in his cheek and a twinkle emanating from his eyes. A wide grin formed, erupting into a burst of laughter and accompanied by a vigorous slap on his thigh.

"You know, there's nothing like a cup of hot coffee to get a guy going in the morning."

Roja's mother scolded him, but she seemed hardly serious in the attempt. When the younger sisters laughed, Roja became angry and used her indignation as an excuse to leave the house.

"I'm going out to unload the wagon and care for the horse. I've got work to do and it's not getting done in here."

With the same twinkle in his eye, Herm the Razzberry Man grinned once more and slapped his thigh.

On the way out the door, Picaro noticed a hammer on the porch table and grabbed it. Since the wheel remained suspended in the air, Picaro quickly removed the keeper pin with the hammer. He worked the seized wheel free after a few minutes. Picaro asked Roja to get him some grease. She welcomed the chance to help. He cleaned and greased the wheel hub and axle shaft. With the wheel mounted and the keeper pin driven back in place, Picaro turned the wheel, doing so until it spun easily. He left the wheel suspended.

When Herm the Razzberry Man came out from the house, Picaro walked to the other side of the wagon. The older man noticed him and asked, "Did you find the wheel that needs fixing? It's the one in the air."

"I know. It's fixed," Picaro answered without looking up.

"It doesn't do much good all jacked up like that."

"No, it doesn't. I just thought you'd like to take a look at it, you know, to make sure it meets with your approval. While I was waiting for you to come out, I thought I'd check a few other things on your wagon. Did you know that the checkreins are dry?"

The young woman's father grinned and said, "Lower the wheel and get the wagon unloaded. I got work to do. Let me know when you're done. I think I got other things for you to do."

"Thank you," said Picaro.

Herm the Razzberry Man did not reply.

Roja grinned at the new farmhand and said, "Picaro, look behind the wagon."

He looked.

She continued, "Do you see that rut in the dirt?"

"Yes."

"Picaro, with your eyes follow that rut to the road and all the way to where it stops. Do you see the point where the rut ends down there?"

"Yes."

"Picaro, that place is where our travels together began."

CHAPTER 18

SHARED LOVE

That autumn the farm and those thereon provided and received many blessings. Herm the Razzberry Man's opinion of Picaro increased. Work for a few days expanded into a handful of weeks. Picaro's desire to be in Roja's presence magnified. Hearing her voice and gazing on her pleased him the most and, as often as permitted, they worked together on the farm. When apart from her for an extended duration, a gnawing ache plagued him as the hours stretched into short eternities. Time with her always seemed brief.

Each night Picaro considered the day gone by. From his makeshift bunk in the barn's loft, his thoughts focused on being with Roja. He wondered how she felt about him. He wanted her to feel the same about him as he felt about her. But did she? Picaro hoped and Picaro doubted.

The longest and most difficult time for Picaro occurred when Roja and her family went to the divine service at the holy place. They had gone thrice since he arrived and each time Picaro refused their invitation to accompany them. Each time, after the family left, he regretted his decision. He remained alone on the farm the entire morning. When Roja and her family returned, they ate lunch. Picaro felt like an intruder. While they spoke of the people at divine service, he perceived himself an outsider.

Picaro determined to accept their invitation the next time, obviously not for the sake of being in the holy place, but rather because he wanted to be with Roja and not remain on the family's fringes. In fact, he realized that by not attending he might lessen his worth in her parents' eyes and that provided additional motivation. Perhaps Roja might become interested in someone else at the holy place.

This would not do. Let the invitation come again and he would quickly accept it. The week passed. The day came. The invitation did not. Early that morning, as on all other mornings when the family went to the divine service, Herm the Razzberry Man bolted the rear seats to the wagon bed. The family departed leaving the farm guest behind. Picaro stood in the doorway of the barn and watched the family until the wagon disappeared from sight.

"No," he suddenly declared to himself, "no invitation is needed."

Picaro began running and while he did not want to catch up to the wagon, he had to regain sight of it. He didn't know the location of the holy place in Water. The cold air clawed deeply into his lungs and made them burn. Shortly he caught a glimpse of the wagon when it turned south and then west again. Picaro ran until he saw the holy place next to a dry, but well-maintained cemetery. Herm the Razzberry Man secured the horse and wagon. By the time Picaro arrived at the entrance to the yard, Roja and her family had entered the building. Picaro slowly approached the holy place, hesitant to enter until he regained his breath, uncertain what he would find within. Other families arrived and entered. Some said hello to the stranger, others smiled their greetings.

A man about Picaro's age stood near the door. No one spoke to the man or looked at him as they entered. When the two of them remained outside the building and the music started, Picaro moved to the main door to enter. The other man shifted a couple steps to intercept him. These actions did not go unnoticed by the war veteran who instinctively readied himself for a confrontation. Repressing the prelude to hostility stirring within him, Picaro stopped and stared at him.

The man spoke, "Are you going in?"

"Yes."

"You hesitate?"

"Because you are in my way."

"No, I meant a moment ago. You hesitated out here. Why are you going in?"

Picaro parried, "Why do people go in?"

He said, "There are many reasons for going in."

"Are you going in?"

Frowning, the man emphatically declared bitterly, "No! Never again!"

Picaro asked, "Well then, do people who are not yet in and who are intending to enter, have to give their reasons for going in especially to someone who remains out and who is never going in again?"

"Point well taken," the man said in a retreating manner. "Sorry. My name is Demas."

"I am Picaro."

"May I ask you a question?"

"Asking is always easy. You may not necessarily get an answer, Demas."

"Has the hound caught you and do you love the Hunter?"

Picaro's brow wrinkled and eyes narrowed as he replied, "The hound is nothing to me and I hate the Hunter! If you want to talk with me, change the subject."

Demas laughed, "Hah! Well spoken. Indeed, comrade, we share the same hatred. But now, my curiosity is piqued. Please tell me why you would go in there?"

"How is that any of your business?"

"It's not really. I'm just interested why someone with such a creed as yours would enter this place."

"A woman I know came to worship here this morning and I want to be with her."

"Ahh, I understand. But be careful in there. The Hunter works situations and uses people to his advantage. His hound is most unscrupulous. You do understand that they may use the woman to catch you?"

"Look, Demas, I heard something a very long time ago. This Hunter, his hound and the wind, whatever the wind is, may be resisted. Is that correct?"

"Yes, Picaro, most certainly true. You are gazing upon living proof of that doctrinal truth. Once I was a member of this holy place. Having been thrice called, I grew up among the people, even serving as the guardian's assistant. I believed it all. I trusted in the hound and loved the Hunter. But something happened to change it all. So, I finally came to my senses. Now, as I am able to resist going into this building, so I can shut out this One. In fact, my friend, there is mounting evidence that the One does not exist. There is no One and there are no Ones."

Picaro did not want to speak about the Other which occupied the dark shadows of his younger years, but he did reply, "You may be correct. I know of One that I thought existed. For awhile I believed I conquered that One. Now, maybe *It* never existed."

Demas added, "Or, like the people in there, *It* exists only in their minds. It is like the make-believe characters we invent in our childish days."

Picaro smiled and said, "Could be, but if that is so, then my conquest over the Other One was no great victory. I have fought nothing but shadows."

"On the contrary, my friend, you have won the greatest victory of all. You have defeated One created by your own mind. The Ones we create, whether in our own image or in the likeness of something else, are always the most difficult. Don't you remember how afraid you were of that One?"

"You are right."

What Demas said made a great deal of sense to Picaro, however something flashed across his mind and he added, "But Demas, does that make the struggle and the terrors any less real?"

A hint of either disapproval or fear passed over the face of Demas who quickly cast it aside and continued, "You better get inside, Picaro. We can talk later. I own the dry goods store in town. Why don't you stop by sometime and we'll talk? I enjoy conversing with you."

"I would like that, Demas. I have to come to town tomorrow."

Picaro opened the door and entered the holy place. While doing so, he heard Demas telling him to be careful.

The holy place did not seem filled to capacity and yet, because those congregated stood as they spoke in unison, Picaro could not see Roja or her family. After several minutes, the assembly sat and began singing a hymn. During the third stanza Picaro located Roja. She sat on the outer aisle about halfway to the front on the left side.

Now came Picaro's huge challenge. The warrior who had fulfilled the sevens had to walk twenty feet up the left side and sit beside the young woman. He waited a moment, and the longer he waited, the more difficult the short journey seemed. He realized the hymn would be over shortly and he wondered when he should walk to the bench where Roja sat. Should he wait until it was quiet and go up? No, he thought it best to proceed forward under the diversion of the singing. Some people would see him, but most, he reasoned, would be looking at their hymnals.

Picaro made his move and started forward. As he did, the people put down the books, sang the "ah yes" and watched the side processional of the stranger. Picaro felt his face flush deeply and cringed internally as many eyes stared at him. He did not have quite enough room to sit beside Roja. She saw him and instant delight radiated from her face. She scooted against her sister who scowled, looked to her left, smiled and scooted to her right. The domino-effect of scowling, looking to the left, smiling and scooting to the right continued until Roja's father received his bump. Unable to scoot to the right because of his position at the center aisle, he did bend forward, took a long, slow, deliberate look to the other end of the bench at his left. The expression on the face of Herm the Razzberry Man did not change.

Roja placed her hand in Picaro's. She filled his mind with thoughts of her and he heard nothing of the proclamation. He did not sing any of the hymns and offered no prayer from either his lips or his mind. For the entire divine service, Picaro focused his attention on the young woman at his side. Though he stared to the front of the holy place, he only pictured her.

After the benediction, final hymn and dismissal, the young woman introduced Picaro to the guardian of the holy place who seemed genuinely pleased to make Picaro's acquaintance. The overseer talked with him briefly before giving him his card.

```
I am David the Ordinator from the
    ancient village of Benedicamus
       at the base of High Mountain.
           I may speak to you.

        (Please keep this card.)
```

Picaro asked the guardian why he hadn't given him another card, one that said the hound was pursuing him. David the Ordinator smiled and answered that it appeared he had already been caught, once by the beloved hound and once by a beautiful maiden.

As they left the holy place, Picaro caught sight of Demas near the wagons. Though their eyes met, no acknowledgment passed between them. As the family approached their wagon, Roja said that she and Picaro would like to walk back to the farm. While her mother said something about it being cold and Roja's younger sisters giggled, the expression on the face of Herm the Razzberry Man never changed.

Roja led Picaro on a short-cut through a wooded area. This was not because she wanted to get home quicker, but rather, so they might enjoy a secluded walk away from the road and the other travelers. They held hands, shared one another's presence and spoke few words. About a third of the way back, they came to a small, dry creek. Picaro jumped across and reached back with his other hand. Roja took it and he pulled her to himself. In doing so, the necklace she wore swung free from her neck and back again. Picaro noticed the necklace and asked her about it. She told him that it was a gift to her. Picaro asked her if she was getting cold. Roja said it seemed to be getting cooler. Picaro used the opportunity to hold her closer as they walked. Arm in arm the couple continued their travels together.

The next day Picaro walked to town. While not the reason he went to town, Picaro did stop at the dry goods store to speak with Demas. They shared many common interests. When Demas asked him if he had been caught by the hound yesterday, Picaro laughed and answered, "Honestly, I didn't hear a word of anything said, sung or prayed. I directed my attention to a beautiful woman."

"Hah! That's what you think. Picaro, you stood there in the presence of -"

Picaro interrupted with mild irritation, "I stood in the presence of Roja."

Demas countered firmly, "No, you stood in the presence of the One. You've got to be careful. You continue what you're doing and you'll be drawn in. Before you know it, you'll be caught. Remember this, you do not choose him. He chooses you. The hound-"

Picaro interrupted him again, "I thought you said the hound wasn't real."

"Be careful, my friend."

The two men talked about various topics for more than an hour. They shook hands and promised to discuss some of the issues soon. As Picaro left, he turned and said, "The hound be with you."

Demas responded in a mocking voice, "Sure. But I won't wish the same curse on you, my friend."

They both laughed, though Demas' laugh fell short of sincerity.

Picaro found the store in town that sold jewelry and bought a silver necklace with a set of intertwined silver wagon wheels. Each end of the clasped chain connected to a wagon wheel.

One afternoon, when the late autumn sun had set, Roja and Picaro took their evening walk. He said to her, "Roja, please accept this necklace as a token of how much I care for you."

She held it to the remaining light. "What are these circles?"

He added, "They are intertwined, Roja."

"They are wagon wheels! This is beautiful, Picaro, not only in the craftsmanship but especially in what it represents."

"Will you wear it in place of your old necklace?"

Roja spoke with sincere anticipation and with no dissatisfaction, "They will be worn together."

Her decision disappointed him, but he succeeded in holding it within himself.

"Tell me about the necklace. It was given to you?"

Willingly she showed it to him and said, "This one is not as shiny as the one you gave to me. It never was. Take a look at it. Can you see what it is?"

Picaro examined it, but the darkness prevented him from making any identification. "Roja, there's not enough light. It's too dark."

"You're right. But look, you can probably make it out if I tell you. It's a miniature trap, like the one in which the Hound died. That's how much he cared for me and that's how much he cares for you, Picaro. And the Hunter sent him forth to rescue us."

"Rescue? I thought the Hunter sent the hound out to pursue the prey. Why the differing opinions?"

"They're not differing opinions; not really. To be rescued one must be pursued."

"I suppose. They mean a lot to you, don't they Roja?"

"Yes. They are the Only One. He loved me and he loves me. First and foremost, I belong to him."

Picaro thought for a long time before speaking softly, "He is your first love. Who am I?"

"You are Picaro. I share my love with you."

"Shared love?"

"When I say that, please believe me, I do not think less of you; I am not lowering your worth. Please listen to me. My parents gave the trap-necklace to me on the day of my *Confessing of the Thrice Calling*. On that day, I confessed the Only One to be my One. I believed then, and I believe now, that the Hunter has a merciful and gracious love for us. I trusted and trust that the Hound has a sacrificial love for us. I am confident that the Blessed Wind has a staying, holy love for me. That is one type of love that no one else is able to give to me. My mother and my father have parental love for me. That is another special love that is not duplicated. But Picaro, there is another kind of love, one that none of the others can give to me."

Roja stopped speaking.

Picaro pondered all these things that Roja said. Finally he asked in a hushed voice, "Roja, does my necklace symbolize the love that none of the others can give to you?"

"Yes."

"Would you wear my necklace too?"

"Yes."

"May I put it on you?"

"Ah yes."

CHAPTER 19

HARVEST SOUGHT, PREY CAUGHT

The thirty-year-old Picaro, veteran of woods and war, trembled at the thought of asking Roja's father for permission to marry his daughter. He did not want to ask because he feared he would not receive permission. He didn't want to delay asking since he wanted to marry Roja before winter. If the truth be known, as far as Picaro was concerned, the ceremony could take place in a matter of days.

After several sleepless nights, he asked the question during breakfast. Herm the Razzberry Man said nothing and his facial expression did not change. Roja's sisters sat still with only their eyes shifting back and forth from their sister to their father. No one spoke during the remainder of the meal. With the last bite of pancake washed down with coffee, Herm the Razzberry Man spoke slowly.

"Roja, go out to the barn and make sure the horse has water."

She retorted, "Horse? Water?"

With a heavy sigh she left. The horse didn't need water, or at least it could wait until after her father spoke. The younger sisters, hoping to behold what came next, remained seated and tried to hide in place. Herm the Razzberry Man dismissed them. Their mother began taking things away from the table. The father of the family got the coffee pot and poured himself half a cup. He walked back to the table and slowly filled Picaro's cup to the brim with the hot, steaming coffee. Picaro winced. Herm the Razzberry

Man replaced the pot and looked out the window above the sink. He gazed upon the brown, lifeless raspberry field to the east of the barn. Picaro waited.

"Does my daughter want to marry you?"

"Yes," he answered eagerly, "but she will not agree to this unless she has your blessing."

Roja's father kept his eyes on the field as if searching for something. After considerable thought, he spoke, "You may marry my daughter when you have learned to sing the *Te Deum Laudamus* and after the berries are all picked from that field."

"Yes sir!" he shouted and quickly asked Roja's mother, "May I be excused? I want to go tell Roja."

Just when Roja's mother started to reply, Herm the Razzberry Man said, "Sure, right after you finish your coffee."

A mixture of emotions came over Picaro. He was elated to receive permission and firmly dejected at having to wait to marry Roja. Still he wanted to run out, find his beloved Roja, tell her the good news, ask her when the berries would be ripe and find out what in the world the *Te Deum Laudamus* was. He wanted to go to sleep and wake up early next summer with the berry harvest home. But before him remained a full cup of hot coffee. He looked at the steaming brew, smiled inwardly and began the slurping process in an attempt to keep from scalding his tongue. When the cup was empty, Picaro hurried outside to find his betrothed.

Herm the Razzberry Man's expression changed. It began with the familiar pinch of snuff placed in his cheek and the characteristic twinkle emanating from his eyes. The wide grin formed, he erupted into laughter and gave his thigh a vigorous slap.

"You know, dear, it's sure good to see the young people today wanting to sing the *Te Deum* and get the harvest home."

Throughout that long winter and into early spring Picaro accompanied the family to the divine service each week. The betrothed couple sat in the same place, sharing a hymnal and holding hands during the service. The order of the divine service never varied and became familiar to Picaro. The structure of the service pleased him and such repetition, combined with the proclamations of David the Ordinator, taught him of the Hunter's love, the Hound's sacrifice and the Blessed Wind's workings.

When they sang the *Te Deum Laudamus*, Picaro closed the hymnal. He and Roja sang it together and felt the unity. Her father and mother sang it together and laughed within. The congregation and her guardian sang it together and rejoiced in the presence of the Only One.

After most services Picaro saw Demas outside the holy place. They made eye contact but never spoke at those times. Picaro did not stop by the dry goods store as often as he had in the first weeks. Whenever Picaro did visit the store, Demas would make strange statements like, "I hate the Hunter for not existing." Saying things like that made Picaro not want to speak with him. He knew he was abandoning Demas and he felt guilty. Demas noticed Picaro's discomfort and told him that the hound had caught him.

One night, as Picaro slept in his bed in the barn's loft, he dreamed a dream. A frantic, commanding voice from within him cried out, "Run, Picaro! Whatever you do, don't stop running."

That's what he ordered himself to do in the dream. The darkened forest stilled in silence and deepened in depth, as the calm before the fury. The high canopy formed by the forest of old growth fir trees filtered the late afternoon light, leaving shadows of shapeless forms. No limb reached out from any tree for a hundred feet above the forest floor. A thick carpet of spongy fir needles made every step an uphill effort and heightened the trapped feeling.

"Run, Picaro, run. Though you hear him not, he is after you. To stop is to die. Run!"

Clouds descended from the tree tops and thick fog billowed onto the forest floor in slow waves. Picaro's world diminished thus decreasing his vision in the direction of his flight.

The closeness of the clouds and the fog allowed the One pursuing Picaro to approach even closer before being seen. The One was present and yet unseen. Picaro knew it.

"Do not turn around and look, Picaro. Run faster!"

He could will his legs to move faster but they would not. His mind and legs churned out of phase while exaggerated movements by his limbs did not increase coordination or reduce clumsiness. The unseen hound bayed in the distance, but where did the howl originate? The sinister fog absorbed the sound and echoed it. The baying originated from every direction and disappeared everywhere. The massive trees blocked the sound as the horde of haunting echoes terminated at all places. For all Picaro knew, he might be running directly at the hound.

"Faster! Get those limbs in sync. He's gaining on you."

Picaro heard a faint cadence behind him. *Ta da dum. Ta da dum. Ta da dum.* Picaro thought of stopping to take a hearing of the sound, but sensed that doing so meant being caught. He would rather die than succumb to the pursuer. *Ta da dum. Ta da dum. Ta da dum.* He ran faster now and more determined. The sound of the hound closed.

"Never give up! Run harder, you fool ... and faster!"

The cadence of the tracker quickened. *Ta da. Ta da. Ta da.* Paws simultaneously striking and scratching the forest floor made the sound. *Ta da. Ta da. Ta da.*

"Run, Picaro."

Ta da. Ta da. Ta da. His blurred eyes made out the edge of the forest. If he could just get by the last ancient tree he would be free. He knew it. He sensed that freedom would be owed to him if he made it past the last tree. This way seemed right to him. As he felt his body coordinate and become more efficient, his sprint quickened. The hound's pace increased. *Ta, ta, ta.* Picaro heard the lungs of the hound heaving behind him. *Ta, ta, ta.* Just as he passed the last tree and began to leave the forest behind, Picaro heard a loud grunt and then, silence -- beautiful, peaceful, *ta, ta, ta*-less silence.

Picaro was victorious. He had conquered. Picaro rejoiced as he continued to run. He could leap and bound and spring and glide. The Other could not leave the woods. The shadowy hound could not cross the line of the trees. He defeated the hound and *It* would dissolve into the darkness and the Hunter would be disappointed. Now Picaro could run forever.

In the same instant that he imagined this freedom, something struck Picaro from behind. The hard blow knocked the wind out of him and hammered him to the stony ground. He tumbled once receiving a severe blow to his forehead from a rock. In the middle of a second flip, the huge dog pinned Picaro on his back. Lily pad sized paws pushed against the crooks of Picaro's elbows and pressed his arms into the earth. The hound's head hung above Picaro's face. Blood freely flowed from the wound on Picaro's forehead. Drool and foam and slobber and spit dangled from both sides of the hound's enormous jowls and wet its prey's face. Super-saturated vapor issued from the beast's nostrils and further fogged the scene. Picaro inhaled this vaporized dog breath. Droplets of water fell from the hound's nostrils and filled the hostage's eyes.

Picaro recovered his breath. His hands and arms were free from his elbows but he could not reach his forehead to wipe the blood and check how deeply he had been wounded. After several feeble attempts to free himself from the hound, he declared a childish, "No fair!"

"Fair, my Picaro?"

The hound's voice was deeper and fuller than the huge animal's size. The sound of his word resonated a depth, fullness and volume greater than what the heavens above could provide. When the hound spoke his name, the word echoed thrice -- once from east to west, once from north to south, and once from below to above.

"Do not ask me to be fair with you, my Picaro."

"No fair! I cleared the edge of the woods."

"Am I bound by my creation, the ancient forest?"

"I was free."

"My Picaro, you were not free."

"Don't call me, *my Picaro*. I do not belong to You."

"You do belong to me. Consider your situation."

"I can resist you."

"I AM Benel the Hound, the One with Crushed Heel, who walks and runs once more and forever. You can only resist me."

"Good. Then I resist you."

"But you are not resisting me."

The man wriggled and pushed, all to no avail.

"I am resisting you now, Benel. I may not be able to do much, but I am resisting you."

"No, my Picaro, you are struggling with me."

"There's no difference."

"Yes, my Picaro, there is a difference, an awful difference, an eternal difference, a blessed difference between resisting and wrestling. If you were resisting me, I could not hold you."

"I choose to resist you. I will to resist you and to be gone, to be far away from you," Picaro declared as he continued struggling.

"Picaro, you are able to make no choice but that of resisting. You did not choose me. I chose you."

"Benel, let my arms go. I want to check my head. It hurts and I am bleeding. If you don't let me go I'll bleed to death."

"No, Picaro, if you resist and leave me, you will bleed to death. The wound you have is a mortal one. Only I can heal you by licking."

The hound lowered his head and reached out with his tongue to lick Picaro's head. The man saw the slobber coming and the spit continuing to drool down upon him. He wriggled and the hound spoke, "Struggling with me is good, my Picaro."

Picaro experienced intense pain as the hound's rough tongue scratched over the surface of his wound. Time after time, the spittled tongue washed through the mortal wound. Picaro cried out during every passing, "Stop, it hurts. You are crucifying me."

Finally he lay still breathing quietly and whispering, "Benel, I struggle no more. I am yours. Do with me as you want."

"My dear Picaro, you will struggle with me again. But you are still mine. Thrice I have called you by name. You are mine. The seal is there, on your forehead."

"You have sealed over my wound?"

"No, just the opposite. I have removed the wound from you and uncovered the seal below it."

"The seal below it?"

"Yes, my Picaro, it is the seal I placed on you in the *Thrice Calling of the Echo*. You bear on your brow the seal of the One with Crushed Heel, who walks and runs once more and forever."

"The seal is still good after all the years away from you?"

The hound's eyes darkened slightly. A deep rumble came from within Benel. "Still good? I AM good. My word was given to you then. My word is as good now as then."

"Time has no effect on you or your word?"

"Am I, or is my word, bound by my creation of time?"

"No, I suppose not."

"Well, why should I, or my word, be limited or suffer decay by the passage of time?"

"You shouldn't, but Benel, why didn't you let me go when I neither knew you anymore nor desired to know you at all?"

"My Picaro, do you think that I will let one go so easily -- one upon whom I have placed my sealing word? No. The pain, suffering, anguish and death brought about when my heel was crushed and held in the trap were not endured to let one like you leave me."

"You could have caught me at any time, couldn't you?"

"Yes and no. Yes, I was capable of doing so, and no, my love for you kept me from doing so."

"Benel, why are you so rough with me? You have taunted me during my days and you have haunted my nights. Why didn't you stop me at another time, in another place or in an easier way than this?"

"Had I done so earlier, you would have resisted me. I had to keep you running, pursuing you but not catching you until now."

"Your pouncing on me was rather harsh wasn't it? I mean, you didn't have to tackle me so hard, did you?"

"Yes, I did. You would have been lost to me had I let you go another stride. One more step and you would have died to me forever. All of my dealings with you, everything from before your beginning to this critical moment, have been necessary."

"Would one more step have been so fatal?"

"Yes, my Picaro. Tilt your head far back and cast your eyes upon your doom."

The back of Picaro's head scraped the ground as he slowly bent his neck. With an upside down view, his eyes beheld certain destruction. In trembling fear he spoke, "The ocean of yellow goo. It's horrible. I'll never get through it to the island. The black shards. I can't even see the island. I am consumed. Woe is me! I am so sorry, holy Benel. I did not do it when I could have, and now I can not do it."

"My Picaro, you never could do it."

" I am lost."

"You are found, for I have done it for you. That is why I have come. The island is yours and I will take you there."

Picaro looked intently and declared sadly, "But I have not been able to see the island since I was a baby." He tilted his head back farther and strained his eyes, "Even now I don't see it."

"This will help you see it," Benel announced and the hound exhaled long and slow. The air cleared and the man beheld the island, "It's beautiful."

"That island is your inheritance, my Picaro."

"How do I get there?"

"I will take you there, but not now. You must do many things for me here on this side first. Later, your time here will end. Then I will then take you to the island, to your inheritance."

"I long for that day. Benel, what are those dark, jagged shards of metal sticking out of the ocean of yellow goo?"

"They are traps. But fear not, for the biggest one, the *Death Trap with the Invisible Hair-Triggered Pan*, is at the bottom of the ocean. I walked onto the ocean and let that monstrous trap ensnare me. The weight of the *Death Trap with the Invisible Hair-Triggered Pan* pulled me down to the abyss and deeper still. I died for the world. But Picaro, I tell you the best now. There, in the depths of destruction, lies the trap that crushed my heel and took my life. The Sea of Death could not hold me. I burst open the trap and from the belly of the ocean I arose. Picaro, I AM Benel the Hound, the One with Crushed Heel, who walks and runs once more and forever."

"Thank you, Benel. Thank you for everything."

"My Picaro, you will struggle with me again."

"Will it be a difficult struggle?"

"More than you can ever imagine, more than is good for you to know now, more than you are able to handle now. But do not worry about tomorrow. Today has concerns enough for you. I will not let you be tempted beyond what strength I give you. In addition, I will provide the way of escape for you."

Picaro breathed in peace and relief, "As You deem necessary, Benel. Please, let me up now, but I ask that you never let me go."

The hound released his hold on Picaro's arms. The man stood and his face felt cool in the breeze. Picaro thought of the slobber from the mouth of the hound. He had hated it before, not so anymore. He said, "Please, Benel, lick not only my forehead, but also my hands, arms, back, and chest. Please, I need such care all over my body."

Benel replied, "He who has bathed does not need to wash. You are clean, my Picaro. I have declared it."

Picaro heard the voice of the Hunter, "This is my Beloved Hound, in whom I am well pleased. Listen to him."

The Blessed Wind blew across the land and into the man's face. Picaro raised his arms against the blast and closed his eyes. Several moments later, all was quiet. Picaro opened his eyes and the hound no longer could be seen. Picaro thought to himself, "Indeed present and yet unseen." He rubbed his face with his hands and discovered the wetness. When he had finally focused his eyes, Picaro realized he was looking at the underside of the barn's roof and that he was in bed and it was the morning of a new day.

CHAPTER 20

AH YES!

Much to Picaro's delight, the warm spring resulted in the berry harvest beginning two weeks early. Picaro started picking berries before sun-up as he labored to get the harvest home. With the early evening chores completed, he grabbed a belly-box and picked until he couldn't see the berries under the bushes. Within the ear range of his future father-in-law, Picaro made comments like, "You know Roja, you better tell your mother to hurry with that wedding dress. We might need it this weekend."

The family continued to harvest the bountiful crop, a task much to the satisfaction of Herm the Razzberry Man. With a twinkle in his eye, but no change in voice, he commented on the bumper crop, purposely waiting until Picaro came within hearing distance before doing so. He boasted to the others as he poked fun at Picaro, saying things like, "Wow! I don't ever remember a bigger crop. The berries just keep coming. It wouldn't surprise me if the season extended three or four weeks. Why, we might even be picking into the fall, shaking the early snow off the last berries."

The mid-summer wedding filled the holy place on a late afternoon. Many of the families from the town of Water and surrounding farms attended. Demas approached the holy place but refused to enter. Picaro and Roja became one when they declared their promise and David the Ordinator spoke the proclamation of the wedding and made the sign of the trap. Those assembled heard the unified confession of the faith when Picaro and Roja sang the *Te Deum Laudamus*.

The family added furnishings to render the barn's loft a suitable place for the couple to live. Roja and Picaro resided in the loft for six years. As their love continued to blossom and grow, they thanked the Hunter for his guidance and care. Each morning they awakened with words of greeting for one another. Each evening as sleep overtook them, they listened to one another's breathing.

The only want unsatisfied was that of children. This unspoken shadow grew darker as the years passed. Roja wept silently in the night petitioning the Blessed Wind to carry her heartfelt desire to the Hunter. Picaro never permitted his tears to surface. Nevertheless, he shed them on the inside, hidden from all save the weeper and the Hunter.

Thus did husband and wife place many petitions and pleas before the Only One who heard their cries and granted their petition. After a particularly cold winter Roja was with child. Joy and gladness warmed a previously unlit place in their hearts. At mid-autumn of their seventh year, the Hunter blessed Picaro and Roja with a son.

A great discussion ensued about the naming of this male child. Herm the Razzberry Man delighted in his first grandchild and put forth the name, Beninu. Picaro's mother-in-law suggested Benhayeel. Roja felt and understood her husband's desire to please her family with a proper name, but she also sensed his frustration as he listened to the many suggestions. She interceded, indicating that the name of the boy would be declared at the *Thrice Calling of the Echo*. She said that even she would not know her son's name until that day when her husband announced it.

The eighth day for the boy coincided with the day of the divine service and the assembly gathered in the holy place. In addition to the traditional twelve Called-Out Candles and the Two Candles of Both Gifts, also the three candles of Holy Calling, the Ear and Sacred Stretching shone brightly among the people. David the Ordinator held the infant boy in his left hand and forearm. The tiny head of Roja's son rested in the wide palm of the guardian's hand.

After the confession of the faith and the singing of the *Te Deum* by father and grandfather, Picaro slipped the white gown over the baby's head and onto his torso and David the Ordinator's arm. The overseer whispered into the tiny ears. The guardian asked Picaro the name of the boy. Picaro spoke the name softly into the ear of David the Ordinator. The holy man smiled when he heard the name and then extended his arms and spoke the baby boy's name loudly.

"BENYONAH!"

The infant did not react. The congregation and the overseer listened for the returning echoes from the high, elliptical ceiling.

"BENYONAH!" "BENYONAH!" "BENYONAH."

Herm the Razzberry Man grinned with admiration, his wife smiled with appreciation, the two sisters sighed and Roja blushed slightly as most in the congregated grinned.

And all the people spoke aloud, "Ah yes."

And Roja whisper-spoke, "Ah yes."

And Picaro said in his heart, "Ah yes."

CHAPTER 21

FAMILY

Benyonah received overflowing love and loved greatly in return. Even at the age of nine, he could remember with fondness the times when rocked in the arms of Roja's mother. As a young baby, he silently named her Grandma Tall One and looked into her eyes as she sang to him. Benyonah revealed this name he fashioned for his grandmother when he formed words and began speaking. Her name was one of his first words uttered. Grandma Tall One smiled when she understand what her grandson had named her.

As soon as the boy walked, Herm the Razzberry Man took him to the farm, particularly the berry fields. There he taught Benyonah the correct cutting of the canes and the proper picking of the berries. The boy watched his grandfather prune the canes and thought it severe. Months later, the boy marveled at the large berries and the bountiful crop.

Benyonah thought that his grandfather was a good storyteller. Herm the Razzberry Man educated the boy with his many tales. On sunny afternoons, the young Benyonah listened to one story after another, until the old man fell asleep. The little boy reclined in the large lap of his grandfather and gazed upward. He peered into those huge nostrils and watched the wild, wiry nose hairs vibrate as his grandfather snored.

Benyonah inherited the eye twinkle from his grandfather and all that came with it. One summer evening, when the boy was seven and the raspberries were ripe, Benyonah smashed twelve overly ripe berries into a squishy mass. Just as it was getting dark, the boy crept to the outhouse. Carefully and quietly, he placed the pulpy mash around the rim of the outhouse seat. Then he went to bed.

The next morning Benyonah and the four adults quietly ate breakfast. The boy had already made his usual early morning trip to the outhouse and saw that someone had already been there and sat on the ripe ring of mashed berries. At the breakfast table, Benyonah flashed glances at the adults as he had opportunity. Grandmother Tall One's dress was not stained as she returned to the stove after bringing a stack of hot cakes to the table. His mother's clothes remained clean. Benyonah knew that the one caught in his trap was either his father or his grandfather. Benyonah waited.

The expression on Herm the Razzberry Man's face did not change. He was stoic and detached. After a heavy sigh, the old man stood up, walked slowly to the stove and took the pot of coffee. When he warmed what was in his cup, he sauntered over to his son-in-law and slowly filled Picaro's cup to the brim. Without lifting his head, Picaro watched his cup being filled and bit his lower lip to prevent either grin or grimace from emerging. Noticing every movement and expression, Benyonah silently watched his grandfather as he returned and repositioned the coffee pot on the hot stove. No stain on the seat of grandfather's pants. The hair on the back of Benyonah's neck bristled.

Herm the Razzberry Man looked outside, sighed once and said, "Kinda cool last night." No one commented. He clucked and stated, "I'm sure glad I didn't have to make a trip down the bunny trail to the outhouse during the dark." No response. "Yup, it sure would've been a chilly experience."

Grandma Tall One questioned innocently, "Was it really that cool last night?"

Roja answered in a short, but obviously uninterested, voice of affirmation, "Probably was."

Benyonah, in a tone and manner revealing his genetic inheritance from his maternal grandfather, yawned and added, "Yea, I hopped down the bunny trail just a few minutes ago. It was a little cool around the edges. It sure must've been even cooler before I got there; I mean, cooler around the edges."

"I'm sure it was, son," replied Roja in her matter-of-fact way of speaking.

Picaro neither moved from his chair nor spoke about the coolness of the night nor commented on the fullness of his cup.

Grandfather slipped the round snuff can from his shirt pocket, tapped the lid twice, opened it and took a pinch of snuff. Speaking slowly from one side of his mouth, he repeated, "Yup, pretty cool last night. If a guy wasn't real careful, he could catch something by having to be outside last night, or even early this morning."

Picaro studied his full, steaming cup in silence.

As grandfather turned to go past the table and outside the house, his eyes met Benyonah's. Both sets of eyes communed in an instant of silent, twinkling laughter. The boy's eyes followed his grandfather as he left the farmhouse. Through the screen door, he watched his grandfather walk to the barn. Halfway across the yard, Herm the Razzberry Man snorted and slapped the thigh of his pant leg.

Benyonah drew a deep breath and asked, "Father, you need a refill on that coffee?"

Without moving his head, Picaro raised his eyes in order to see the hint of a smirk on the boy's otherwise innocent face. Picaro ran his tongue across the underside of his front teeth and shook his head slightly in the negative.

Benyonah announced he was going out to the barn to see if his grandfather needed any help. A few steps outside the house, the boy slapped the thigh of his pant leg.

A puzzled expression formed on the face of Picaro's wife as she panned from her son to her husband. "What was that all about?"

Picaro did not reply. He sipped from his hot cup of coffee but could not prevent a dribble from going down his shirt.

Roja manifested her love for her son in many wise and patient ways. She hymned the ancient songs of the Hunter. Tune and text fed the boy's soul from before the earliest of his days. Benyonah learned the orations to the Only One before he could speak the words. She read many books to the boy, especially the old books. Benyonah's mother loved her son enough to correct him. She spanked him when he needed it, but always in a way and to a degree that demonstrated her concern for him. Since she sought only to discipline him, she never punished him.

Roja held him securely and spoke words of comfort after a bad dream. Booming thunder always scared the boy and while still young he sought and received refuge in the arms of his mother. The side of his head pressed tightly against her bosom while one of her hands covered his outside ear. At such times, Benyonah would close his eyes and listen. His mother shielded the muffled thunder and he focused his hearing to her sounds; to the beating of her heart and her breathing. These resonations from within, that surrounded him for nine months when the boy lived and grew within his mother, comforted him and gave him a sense and feeling of security and safety.

Picaro loved his only son intensely. He feigned defeat as he let Benyonah overpower him in wrestling matches. He taught the boy the value of patience, perspective, self-control, work and self-discipline. The father laughed at, with and near his son when they played and worked together.

As the boy grew older, Picaro became immersed in silent reflection for lengths of time and with a manner of expression that his son noticed. Picaro's mood changed and he often appeared distant to his son. The father's face expressed a coolness that did not go unnoticed by either Roja or Benyonah. The man raised in the woods lived in painful awareness that a father might not always be with his son. While no possibility existed that Picaro would fall into Mac's habit of drinking, a transgression which left the boy without a father, Picaro considered the many other reasons why a son might have to grow up without his father at home. Accidents happen. Wars break up families. Innocent bystanders are killed. Diseases consume. Picaro knew that he might be called by the Hunter while his son was still quite young. He did not desire to leave his son but the Only One's will might be contrary to the desires of a father.

The seasoned warrior wanted his son to be ready to live without him and he prepared the boy for his father's death. He taught him about dying and about living. They talked about people who died, like Jack the butcher upon whom a swarm of bees descended and stung him to death. Jack left behind his wife and four children, the youngest close to Benyonah's age.

Picaro posed situations to the boy and asked him hypothetical questions. There were times when the boy asked his father for an answer and Picaro said, "You think about it and come up with the answer. You might as well start doing now what you will be expected to do later. How would the Hunter have you think?" Or he would say, "Benyonah, those are the kinds of questions you are going to have to ask and answer yourself." Sometimes Picaro's son asked for help with some work around the farm and Picaro told him, especially as he grew older, "Think about it son, and try to get it done. Look at the situation from different viewpoints. Don't take it apart until you understand how it fits together. Figure things out. I trust you can do it." Or he would say, "Benyonah, those are the kinds of things you are going to have to do for yourself."

Once at the end of breakfast and just before Benyonah tried to repair a farm gate, the boy asked, "Father, why do you make me think and do for myself? With you helping me it makes things a lot easier."

His father replied, "One day you will be a man with a wife and children. You will be the head of the family. Your children will need to know that they are loved and cared for by you and your wife. Decisions that you make will have to be for their benefit and care. When they come to you for help, they will need to know that they can count on you."

"Don't worry, father, they will be able to trust me," Benyonah replied. A mischievous, Herm-the-Razzberry-Man twinkle formed in his eyes. Without asking, he went to the stove, got the coffee pot, filled his father's cup to the brim, returned the pot to the stove and said, "Father, I promise you this. If my little boy comes to me with a question I will tell the poor little fellow, 'My son, that is the kind of question you are going to have to start answering for yourself.'"

As the young man finished his declaration, he walked out the door laughing. "Finish your coffee," he shouted as he began running. Picaro took off in quick pursuit, promising to catch him and work him over with a good tickling.

Continuing to laugh as his young legs stretched in full escape, Benyonah shouted back, "You can't catch me, father!"

Even though the middle-aged Picaro announced, "Oh yes I can," on that day the father could not catch the son. At the end of the corral stood Herm the Razzberry Man who, with his eyes twinkling, put a pinch of snuff inside his lip, laughed out the side of his mouth and slapped his thigh.

Except for the blizzard in Benyonah's seventh year and the great fire in the ninth summer of the boy's life, the family went to the holy place every week. The five stood together to make their *Confession of the Transgression.* When David the Ordinator announced the *Word of the Blood Hound's Cleansing*, the three generations chanted the *Ah yes.* After the reading from the *Chronicles of the Only One*, the congregation hymned the ancient lyrics. Indeed, the high abyss in the arched heavens received the haunting echo of the *Te Deum Laudamus* sung by the holy assembly throughout the centuries and most recently by the family of Benyonah.

On the day of Benyonah's *Confessing of the Thrice Calling*, the young man received many gifts. Not one, however, was as intriguing as the one he received from his grandfather. The family gathered around the table feasting on the traditional meal. Benyonah opened the beautifully wrapped presents from his two aunts. One aunt gave him an old book, *Tales of the Little People from the North*. The other aunt presented him with a large hunting knife. Benyonah also gladly received a shirt from Grandma Tall One, a worn hymnal from his mother and a leather pack made by his father. Herm the Razzberry Man reached into his large pocket and took out a small object crudely wrapped in paper from a used brown sack. Benyonah received it in hand and thanked the giver. The sack was very light, almost no weight to it at all. The young man carefully removed the outer layer of paper. In his hand he held one of his grandfather's snuff cans. He twisted the lid off the small can and discovered nothing inside. A twinkle formed in Benyonah's eyes as he looked up at his grandfather.

"It's empty, grandfather."

The old man's eyes contained no twinkle and he said in a dreadfully serious tone, "That's right, Benyonah. Do not forget that it is empty. The trap crushed him and we killed him, but neither death nor the crypt could hold him. The tomb is empty."

Benyonah spoke, "Thank you, grandfather. This I will treasure."

Herm the Razzberry Man asked in reply, "You will treasure an empty can?"

With no hint of a twinkle in either eye, the son of Picaro answered, "No, I will always treasure the truth of the empty can."

CHAPTER 22

LIFE SEARCHING AND SOUL SEARCHING

Following the gathering at the holy place, whenever the weather permitted, Roja and Picaro walked the way known as Roja's Short-cut. The tradition continued after Benyonah's birth. The boy joined the walk, first bundled in blankets and arms, later hoisted on the shoulders of his father and finally, as Herm the Razzberry Man often said, "riding on shanks' mares."

One early spring day following the divine service, a time well after Benyonah's *Confessing of the Thrice Calling*, the family of three returned by way of Roja's Short-cut. Halfway along the walk, Roja noticed her son's silence. The usual explorations of the boy's outside world had given way to reflective investigations. Roja wondered if Benyonah might be ill, or perhaps he had an important matter to consider?

She asked, "Are you sick?"

"No, mother, I am well."

He continued his silent walk, remaining ten or fifteen feet ahead of them. Roja squeezed Picaro's hand and drew nearer to his ear, "Something is troubling our son."

"He said he wasn't sick."

"I know, but that doesn't mean something isn't the matter with him."

Picaro whisper-spoke, "Well, he can work it out for himself or he may seek help from us. He will let us know."

"He is letting us know."

Picaro intended his whisper-speaking to be heard only by his wife. However, Benyonah's youthful ears heard what he said. The young man smiled at the ground in front of him and continued walking.

Several minutes later Roja inquired, "Do you need some help with something, Benyonah?"

The young man stopped and turned to his parents, "Yes, and I am not able to resolve the matter by myself."

"Is it something only one of us may help with?"

"No, it will take both of you."

His mother offered, "We're here and we're listening, if this is a good time to speak of this matter."

"Okay. ... Well, I could not have asked for a better mother or father. My life has been one in which you have given me all that you believe I needed. You have provided me with clothing and shoes, meat and drink, house and home, and much more than others have. You have raised me in the holy place and I do not remember a time when I did not know the Only One. Grandfather and grandma love me, and I love them too. I am a member of the family and perhaps a bit spoiled since I am your only child and their only grandchild. But something is missing."

Benyonah hesitated a moment and Picaro spoke with bewilderment and the slightest hint of sharpness, "I do not understand. What are you speaking about? What could you possibly be missing?"

His mother spoke, "I believe I know what it is. It is something that I am missing as well, isn't it son?"

Benyonah cast his eyes down in momentary hesitation, then slowly raised them as he spoke, "I have not thought about it from your perspective, but yes, mother, I guess it is true for you as well."

Picaro remained puzzled and more frustrated as he alone wondered. With a trace of anger he asked, "Well, please tell me what it is that you and your mother are missing?"

His son answered, "I know only half of my family. My other grandfather is veiled in silence and therefore is a mystery. You have never spoken to me of him and I would like to know about him and meet him. I have never seen my other grandma and she has never seen me. Those two people are the parents of my father and my father is a good man. I would like to know and meet and talk with my father's parents. That is what I am missing, father."

"My beloved Picaro, our son speaks well for himself, but not for himself only, but also for me."

The head of the family remained silent.

The young man continued, "I mean, I wonder what my other grandfather is like? Does he have a name? What kind of a laugh does he have? What of my grandma, does she know I exist? Would she like to meet me?"

Picaro slumped his chin to his chest and closed his eyes.

Roja spoke as softly and sincerely as she could, "Benyonah, those are the kinds of questions your father is going to have to answer. Let's walk on ahead for a little while."

Picaro wept.

Later in the darkness of that night, neither Roja nor Picaro could sleep in their bed in the loft. Roja said quietly to her husband, "Shall we talk?"

With a weariness that comes only when struggling with one's soul, Picaro sighed and said, "What would you have me say, dear wife?"

She answered in a calm voice, "Only what you have not said since we met."

He sighed and said, "It is all a part of my past, almost a past life that never was. For so many years I wandered about with no purpose, as a boy and as a warrior. Only after I came here and met you and your family did I discover a purpose for being and did my life have meaning. Here the Hound finally caught me. Here my life began. The times before, the times of his pursuit as well as the ordeals I lived through earlier are not something I wish to recall. So, I've not spoken of them. Those things are painful."

"Your father? Tell me of him."

"I have a difficult time speaking of him as my father. His name is Mac. I remember him as being tall and strong. Mac's arms were huge from working in the woods and sawmills. On those rare occasions when he played and wrestled with me, Mac lifted me up as if I weighed nothing. But Mac deserted my mother, my two brothers and me. Those in the dens of strong drink saw more of him than we did. The money needed for his family's food and care he spent on strong drink. I came to hate Mac and I am not sure my opinion is any different right now. He abandoned us and made my mother's life miserable and hard. He left my life when I was a small boy and he never came back. He could have found us if he wanted and he didn't. We were not that important to him for all those years. So my mother continued without a husband and my brothers and I grew up without a father. I have lived my life without Mac, without a father and am now quite happy, having been blessed by the Only One. I have gone for months and maybe even years at a time without thinking about him."

"Benyonah thinks about him."

"I know."

"Tell me of your mother."

"She is a great woman of remarkable strength and mental determination. Her name is Eliza and she gave herself for us boys. When Mac left it seemed that she gathered us under her wings and would have defended us to the death. Most of what she had was gone but her sons would not be taken from her. During some seasons, she worked two jobs. Day after day, when she got home from the second job, she cooked food, washed clothes, ironed shirts and made certain we had what we needed. All the while, my brothers and I slept. It must have been a tremendous burden of physical strain, mental stress and a constant emotional drain. Looking back on it, there is no doubt in my mind that she never thought of herself."

"Why wouldn't you want your son to meet her?"

Picaro did not answer.

Roja waited several minutes and then put her arms around his neck, held him tightly and spoke gently to him.

"I am going to ask you a question. You are not to answer it to me. Keep it to yourself. In asking it, my beloved husband, I am not condemning you or making any judgment against you. I think you need to hear the question and consider it in your own mind. Picaro, your father abandoned your mother; how are you any different than your father?"

Picaro's muscles tensed and his body shook, but he did not speak. Roja held her husband closer still, but said no more. Tears of contrition poured forth from the man while tears of sympathy streamed from his wife. Hours later Picaro felt his wife's arms slip from around him as she fell asleep. She was a great blessing to him and he loved her more than ever that night. He thought of the Hunter, his mother, the Hound, Mac, the pursuit, Dave, his son, the holy place, his wife, Anton, the dream, Grandma Tall One, the future, Herm the Razzberry Man, the Holy Wind, Demas, the Only One's will and his own will. He heard his wife's breathing against the stillness of the night. Hours later weariness overcame him and he slept.

The next evening after the supper meal, Picaro asked his wife and son if they wanted to make the long trip to visit the place where he was born and raised. Benyonah burst out with an immediate "yes!" Roja nodded her head joyfully and smiled at her husband.

Picaro indicated that the long journey would take more than two months to get there and two more to return. He could not say how long they might stay in the area. More than twenty years passed since he had seen his mother. Picaro confessed that he did not really know where his mother was living, or for that matter, if she was even alive. He told his son, in front of the others, that he had transgressed greatly in these matters and he looked to the Hound for forgiveness. Picaro told the family that he had not been a good example for Benyonah because he had not cared for his mother as he should have. After Picaro finished speaking, Herm the Razzberry Man told his grandson that Picaro had given a good example of how to admit transgressions to others and seek restoration from the Only One who pardons abundantly.

Two days later the three prepared to leave on the long journey. They packed only the essentials, only what they could carry on their backs - a blanket for each, an extra pair of boots, dried fruit, some jerky, a small pan, matches and extra clothing. Picaro reckoned they would be back no sooner than six months and no more than a year. The elderly couple assured them that everything would be waiting for them when they got back.

Benyonah could not contain his excitement. The "great trek to the woods of the north and west" would be the adventure of the boy's life. He placed the treasured snuff can in his pack and strapped the hunting knife to his hip. He inhaled Grandma Tall One's early morning breakfast. As they stepped out the door, Benyonah's father produced his warrior's hat from the Side of the Sun and placed it on his son's head.

Roja kissed her parents good-by. As she hugged her, Roja's mother secretly placed a small packet into Roja's hand. Neither said anything about the transaction. Picaro shook hands with his wife's parents. In the greatest expression of affection he could muster, Herm the Razzberry Man slapped Picaro on the back as they shook hands. With a twinge of suspicion, Picaro wondered what might have been placed on his back. Benyonah gave warm hugs and kisses to his grandparents and told them he'd be back soon.

Such farewells, ones where there is an anticipated return in the not-too-distant future, are tearful and difficult but not traumatic. The good-byes that wrench the soul are the ones that are final on this earth and extend to eternity. As the trio began the walk around the turn where the two grandparents could no longer be seen, they had no idea that the good-byes just spoken were their final ones with these two old people.

Not one of them would ever see Grandmother Tall One or Herm the Razzberry Man again ... at least, in this life.

CHAPTER 23

WISDOM FROM OF OLD

The open farmlands gradually gave way to a vast prairie. The terrain allowed a gentle transition as their bodies, particularly the feet of the adults, acclimated to the long journey. Many muscles made their presence known and voiced objection to the new and prolonged strain.

An unnoticed and gentle incline foretold the advent of mountains. Prairie grasses yielded to sage and scrub brush. Sources of water became scarce as the bushy landscape stubbornly gave way to hills with random outcropping of rock. The distant mountains crept closer as walking evolved into hiking. In the third week, the air thinned and became sharper as the three climbed the slopes of the mountain range. Their daily traveling distance decreased from twenty miles to five miles. As the temperature dropped, they wore warmer clothes and soaked up the warmth of the night fires. The howling of wolves joined the night barking of lone coyotes.

Dark green patches of hardy evergreen trees signaled the crossing of the mountain divide. Snow fields testified to more moisture on the west side of the great mountain range. Old snow remained frozen solid until the afternoon sun began to turn the top inch into slush. While pitchy knots for fire became more abundant, dry wood became scarce.

One late afternoon in the fourth week, the seasoned woodsman and retired warrior felt strangely uneasy. As the threesome crossed a large, open snowfield, Picaro's eyes ranged the landscape and scoped the horizon. He sensed that they were being watched and perhaps followed. Rocks, shadows, contrasts and scattered trees prevented Picaro from locating the predator.

Instinctively, Picaro made a quick assessment of resources and terrain. In a normal voice, he told his family to veer slightly to the left and to pick up the pace. He began directing them to an oasis of evergreens two hundred yards away. Picaro walked at a slower pace and listened carefully as he went. He told his wife and son to walk faster. Several times he saw shadowy flashes of dark brown to his right. Above him and to the right he detected a movement. His peripheral vision caught a silhouette against a patch of snow. A couple minutes later, he turned and walked backwards. He scanned the broken snowfield to the east and saw three figures in the distance. Picaro now knew the danger, a pack of wolves had been following them and were now closing for the kill.

He turned back and quickened his pace to catch-up to his wife and son. The sun approached the horizon and it would not be long before the darkness of night consumed the mountain and its inhabitants. Wife and son, still unaware of any danger, were within fifty yards of the trees. Picaro checked the area above and behind him. At least two animals began trotting directly at them from above. Three, possibly more, loped at their quarry from behind. A direct look to the left revealed no sign of a wolf. The pack behind them began its attack run. The chase, designed to isolate one victim and run it down, commenced. Picaro directed his family in a path that caused him to be the victim. The two elements of the pack would converge on their prey at the same time.

Picaro slipped his arms from his large pack and let it drop to the ground behind him. He kept walking about five feet behind his wife and son. In a calm and stern voice, he commanded them emphatically, "Don't stop walking. Do not turn around. Do exactly as I tell you. We are in great danger. Keep walking and slip out of your packs. Do it now."

They did as told. Roja asked, "What is it?"

Her husband ignored her question. "Son, take your knife out of its shield and hand it back to me. Do not turn around. Both of you keep walking quickly to those trees. When you get there, climb the trees as high as you can. Hurry. We don't have much time."

Benyonah handed the knife to his father. Roja repeated her question.

"Wolves," he answered, "at least five of them, probably more. Now run as fast as you can and climb one of the trees. Run! I will be right behind you. Run and climb. Don't look back."

Mother and son ran for the safety of the trees. In a matter of seconds they closed the distance to the eight inch diameter trees and began to climb the lower branches in their attempt to reach a safe height.

Picaro fingered the large hunting knife and glanced over his shoulder. The wolves had cut the distance in half. He shed his coat and rolled up the left sleeve of his shirt. With the tip of the sharp knife, he made a small cut on the back of his exposed arm. His blood dribbled from the wound. Picaro drew the sharp edge through the flowing blood from its tip to the hilt. When ten feet from the trees, he forced the handle into the snow leaving the blade with its bloody edge exposed. With his boot, Picaro scraped more icy snow to the knife and compacted it with his foot. Both treed humans pleaded with him to hurry. Having scraped and compacted the snow three more times for the burial and securing of the handle, the bloody blade stood solidly erect in the surface of the snow, the blood already beginning to freeze in place. As Picaro moved from the exposed knife blade and to his tree, he saw that the wolves behind him had stopped momentarily to investigate the packs and his coat.

Before he reached the same height as his wife and son, the wolves were below. Picaro looked from his tree and could see the area away from the trees but not directly below. He asked them how many wolves they saw coming. Benyonah said he saw three running from the way they came. Roja did not see any of the ones from the hill to the right, but confirmed the three.

The late afternoon shadows cast by the trees, combined with the numerous layers of boughed limbs between them and the ground, made seeing the wolves below nearly impossible. Sounds filtered through needles and limbs. Only small patches of fur were momentarily visible. Picaro heard breathing and scratching sounds. The pack below was sniffing the base of the tree and searching for the treed prey.

The running about stopped. A snarl met a growl. A yip preceded a breathing sound. A yelp led to two growls and the noises escalated. Vicious snarls led to a canine cacophony as the low tones of growls preceded high-pitched barks and ripping snaps. The horrid individual sounds of the wolves combined and blended into a din of chaotic pandemonium. Killing shrieks, death-dealing bites, lethal snaps and savage snarls revealed the frenzied battle waged below. Bodies slamming against one another as wolf rose up against wolf. At its height, Picaro imagined the hideous cries ascending from perdition at the bottom of a fiery abyss.

The frenzy below lasted less than ten minutes. The battle amongst many evolved into single matches between combatants. From their perches, the trio heard sounds in isolated spots. One fight took place directly at the base of Picaro's tree. Two, possibly three wolves savagely tore at one another up the slope from the trees. Another pair waged a death battle slightly to the east.

Mortal wounds evoked monstrous screams that subsided to distinct death rattles or gulps of air through gaping throat wounds. The victor below the tree and winner to the east paired off against each other. The sound of death was heard up the slope. The fight continued there as a head-to-head match ensued. Shrieks followed loud snarls and sudden whines followed mortal bites.

Picaro motioned for his son and wife to remain quiet. Two wolves remained below. Though both had been mortally wounded, they were driven by the blood lust of animals fighting for survival. Each animal circled the other, one hobbling on three legs, the other with its head inclined to the side because of a gaping neck wound. Each rested for new energy and sought an opening for the slashing bite that would kill the other. One wolf did not move well and it yelped in its painful attempt not to be flanked. The other wolf, no doubt suffering the effects of substantial blood loss, watched for its opportunity. After several moments one of the beasts charged into the other. Final growls and bites were exchanged as one wolf executed the death gnash.

Movement ceased below the trees and the sounds decreased to an occasional whimper. Ten minutes later, Picaro, Roja and Benyonah heard nothing more below them.

"I am going down a ways. Maybe I'll be able to see what is left," said Picaro in his normal voice. He climbed down. "Stay there," he ordered as he descended.

Back on the ground, Picaro surveyed the slaughter. He retrieved Benyonah's knife and began checking each fallen animal. A feeble growl came from a still body. With a quick, precise stick, Picaro put the animal out of its pathetic existence.

"You can come down."

While the two climbed down, Picaro retrieved their packs and returned as mother and son surveyed the grizzly scene.

"Here is your knife, son. Let's get our packs on and move from here."

"Gladly," replied a shaken Roja, "but what happened?"

"Yes," chimed in Benyonah, "why did they kill each other?"

Picaro hurried along as the sun dipped below the horizon. He motioned to an area of bare ground a quarter mile off and stated, "We have just enough time to make it to the clearing and start a fire for the night."

While they walked, he explained the situation.

"I'm not exactly certain. Wolves don't normally act this way. The pack, or packs, of wolves had been following us for some time. We had no chance of outrunning them and even if we made it to the trees, we couldn't stay treed for long."

"No," said Roja, "I can't imagine being able to stay up that tree all night."

Picaro continued, "The winter must have been hard on these desperate beasts. Hunger drove them and we had only one option. I made a small cut on my arm and put the blood along the sharp edge of the blade. I forced the handle into the snow and compacted the icy snow to make it secure. One of the wolves quickly found the bloody knife and began to lick it. The blade slit its tongue. I thought they would individually bleed to death as each continued to lick first the blood from the knife and then its own blood. I never anticipated what happened. These beasts must have lost their dominant wolf or had became so hungry that they refused to be put off. Whatever the situation, with the blood lust of the wolf triggered, the first wolf's own bleeding urged it on and, at the same time, attracted the others. The pack attacked the injured and bleeding wolf and eventually one other. New blood flowed from the animals as they turned on each other. A deadly, fighting frenzy ensued and you heard and now see the result."

Benyonah asked, "How'd you know to do what you did?"

"An old woodsman who hung around the sawmill often told me stories about life in the forests of the north. This trap for the wolves was one of those stories, but as I said, what happened here is puzzling to me."

Roja suggested, "Maybe they had rabies."

"I don't know."

"I'm glad you remembered that old story," said his son, adding, "I have a quick-thinking father."

"Benyonah, I'm thankful that your grandfather took the time to sharpen your knife to such a fine edge."

Roja added, "I'm thankful to the Hunter for watching over us and delivering us."

Later that evening, the three huddled around a warm fire, soaking in the heat and staring into its burning center. With the cracking and popping of pitch knots burning and the sparks ascending as the fire snapped, each member of the family sat deep in thought and prayerful thanksgiving. As the fire died down, Benyonah shared his meditation.

"Certain death faced us and the only thing that saved us was the spilling of blood. Shed blood is what saved us; shed blood is what defeated our enemy."

Several moments later, Picaro announced, "I have a wise son."

CHAPTER 24

POSSIBILITIES

The dispersed sentinels of hearty noble fir in the high elevations gave way to stands of pine and hemlock as the trio descended. High lakes with brushy vegetation yielded to meadows of lush grass. Lavender lupin reached for the sun in open fields while white trillium lit up deep forests. Roja marveled when her eyes first saw the yellow johnny-jump-ups and the white peppermint flowers growing along the mountain streams. She regretted not having a book to press and preserve the flowers as she picked several blossoms and hoped to find more on the trek home. In this land of discovery, Benyonah climbed, swung and bounced on the springy branches of large vine maples.

After walking and viewing the open spaces of the higher elevations, the family was forced to travel single file through the woods. Picaro located animal trails and followed them through the underbrush and along the creeks. In the mountains they could see for miles in every direction. Now, amidst the woods and brush, visibility was limited to a few feet. When emerging at a cliff or impassable valley, they backtracked. More rain fell on the western slopes than on the other side of the mountain and the dampness soaked them. A steady drizzle came down as they tromped through soggy woods, their thoughts turning to the warmth and food of home. They had been on half-rations for a week now and as they plodded along they thought of Grandma Tall One's breakfasts and the hot coffee of Herm the Razzberry Man. Hours passed when they did not speak.

Their spirits lifted one foggy morning when they happened upon an overgrown wagon road, the first sign of humanity seen in weeks. Loggers or miners abandoned the road years ago. Now stands of alder, more than fifteen feet high, grew between the salal-covered ruts. Following the road for a mile, the three came to an open area with several deserted shacks. The weathered, gray huts, nearly overgrown with blackberry vines, offered respite for the weary troop. Though short of food, the family decided to stay in one of the shacks for a few days, giving them time to dry out and warm up. After overcoming the difficulty of finding enough dry wood, father and son started a fire and Benyonah occupied his time in keeping it kindled. There were no pitch knots to be found and what wood he did locate outside was wet. As a result, they used the drier floor boards of the other shacks for the fire.

Two days later the skies cleared and the family left the shelter. The old road led to a large field. After crossing the open land, they came to the top of a rise overlooking a valley. Benyonah excitedly pointed to a town in the distance. In the early afternoon they passed remote houses and late in the day, arrived in the small town. Picaro learned from a shepherd that they had entered a town aptly named, Quaking Aspen Pass. Though there was no inn, they secured a warm room for the night from one of the residents. The peripatetic family thanked the Hunter for having safely guided them and they ate a humble, yet most satisfying meal with a woodcutter and his family.

The next day was the day of the divine service and the family hoped to locate a holy place in the small town. As there was none in the small town, Picaro led the others in family devotions in the house where they spent the night. The three relied on their memory for the order of service, the reading and the singing of the hymns. The host family, for the first time, heard the good news of the Hound and marveled at the Hunter's love. The woodcutter thanked Picaro and his family for sharing the great mystery with them.

While everyone in the town spoke with them in a friendly manner, no one in Quaking Aspen Pass had ever heard of Woods Town or Upper Woods Camp. After staying two days in the pleasant town, Picaro, Roja and Benyonah traveled farther west and after walking four more days and passing through several villages, they reached a larger town called River Birch Bend. From his youth, Picaro had a vague recollection of having heard of this town, but he could not be certain. As they walked Picaro asked about the old names. A mute pointed north and wrote on the ground with a stick, informing him that the town of Cedarville was more than 80 miles to the north.

Picaro and family began the journey north the following day. In the afternoon of the second day, they entered a town and beside the roadway a dark-haired man motioned them to come to him. They did so and he gave them a card.

```
I am Timothy the Liturgist from the
    ancient village of Benedicamus
    at the base of High Mountain.
        I may not speak to you.
   (Please return this card to me
        after you have read it.)
```

Picaro smiled, gave the card back to him and said, "I am most pleased to meet you, Timothy the Liturgist. May the Only One be with you."

A broad grin came across Timothy the Liturgist's face and he motioned his acknowledgment of the greeting and used his hands to return it in kind.

Picaro asked, "Do you have another card for me?"

Timothy the Liturgist returned the smile and shook his head in the negative.

Picaro was surprised and remarked, "Why not? I thought you and those like you always gave out a second card?"

Timothy the Liturgist smiled and handed another card to Picaro.

> *The Hunter is after you.*
> *The Wind has given your scent*
> *to His Hound.*
> *At this very moment*
> *His Hound is tracking you.*

Picaro chuckled and said, "I understand. Since I already belong to the Hunter, I don't need this card."

Timothy the Liturgist nodded his head in the affirmative. Picaro turned the card over and read the other side.

> *The sophia-ists have put out the hex,*
> *For those who ordain based on sex.*
> *So they cast out the hym-nal,*
> *And reeled in a her-nal,*
> *It's "okay" say ecclesial execs.*

Picaro's face turned slightly grim. "Here you are wrong, my friend. I need this card. False doctrine and practice should not be permitted in the holy places. Only qualified men are to be guardians. Were you the guardian of the holy place in this town?"

Timothy the Liturgist's countenance fell as he nodded his *yes*. He glanced at Picaro's family and looked back at Picaro.

"I'm sorry, this is my beloved bride, Roja and our son, Benyonah."

Timothy the Liturgist extended his hand to them and greeted them warmly. He motioned all of them to follow him. He led them across several streets, through an alley and into an old one-room house. After closing the door, he said, "Please, sit down, my friends."

Benyonah and Roja were astonished and the boy asked, "I thought you couldn't speak?"

Picaro laughed.

"It is the difference between *can* and *may*. I can speak, but I may not speak. I am perfectly capable of speaking as you now know. However, according to the rulers of this town, I no longer have permission to speak the proclamation. Speaking is something I may not do."

Roja asked why.

"I am forbidden to speak anymore because, as a faithful guardian of the holy place, I spoke only of the Hunter, the Hound and the Wind - the Only One. Both those within and those without the holy place exerted great pressure on me to be more tolerant. Many, and tragically almost everyone, wanted me to allow the worship of other ones in the holy place. They wanted to take away the singing of the ancient songs and the old teachings. I refused and spoke that the only way to eternal rest was through Benel, the Blood Hound with Crushed Heel, who walks and runs once more and forever. I tried to tell them of the freedom of dogma and the tyranny of tolerance. This infuriated them. They rose up and cast me out of the holy place, removing me from the office of guardian, forbidding me to speak and convincing the ruling authorities to pass and enforce laws against my speaking as well."

Picaro asked, "Is this true of all the other guardians who are not permitted to speak?"

"Probably," Timothy the Liturgist replied. "Why? Have you met some of my brother guardians who have been so silenced?"

"Yes, long ago. Tell me, overseer, why do you remain in this place?"

"I am the guardian here."

"Do you have any people that you oversee?"

"No, they have all been persuaded to join the other side. The last faithful member died three weeks ago. For that dear person I wanted to officiate at the *Ceremony of Returning the Clay,* but I was not permitted. The voters' assembly forbade it. Now I have no one left to care for," he announced sadly, but added with hope, "unless you three are staying here?"

"No, we are traveling to the north where I was born and raised," Picaro replied. "Please, I don't think that you should stay here. There is need for guardians in other places. Kick the mud from your boots and go."

"Where would I go?"

"Go south to River Birch Bend. Then walk east until you come to Quaking Aspen Pass. It is a small town where the decaying effects of tolerance have not eroded the backbone of the people nor poisoned their minds with the venom of pluralism. Men, women and children work hard and we were received well by everyone. Ask for the house of the woodcutter. He and his family will welcome you and help you get started. There is no holy place, so both opportunity and hard work await you."

Excitement, anticipation, resolve and a renewed sense of purpose erupted from Timothy the Liturgist's manner and words.

"I am leaving this day, within the hour. I have very little to take with me. The people here burned all my books and papers. Only because it was with me at the time they raided this house was my copy of the sacred volume spared from the fire. If you want, you may stay here tonight."

Picaro said, "No, we will be on our way. We were only passing through when we met you. Besides, it seems as if this is not where we would be welcomed by any residents except you."

The guardian spoke, "Former resident. I have already left. If you travel to the north, you may want to stay in the next town, Oak Fork. You will have just enough time to get there before dark. Find the holy place in town. Behind the holy place is the small house of Manoah the Lector. Tell him I sent you. He will give you lodging for the night. Please extend my greetings to him in the Name of Benel and tell him of my plans to proclaim the Only One in Quaking Aspen Pass."

"Manoah the Lector?"

"Yes," replied Timothy the Liturgist, "Yes, but I must leave. Likewise, if you desire to arrive in time, you must go."

"Wait," commanded Picaro taking out a pouch, "you will need some money to get yourself settled and going at Quaking Aspen Pass."

He poured out many gold coins from his pouch. For every nine he put back, he slid one over to the guardian. After more than twenty gold coins had passed over to the guardian, he responded in astonishment, "Sir, you have not known me for more than an hour and do you simply hand over so many gold coins to me?"

"You are our brother. My wife, my son and I are asking you to let us help you in a small way to begin the work in the town of Quaking Aspen Pass. We are doing the easy thing by offering gold for this work. Yours is the more difficult; you are devoting your life to this work."

"May the Hound announce the well-spoken word to all of you on the day of the Curtain Pulling! Please remember me in your intercessions. I will include your names in my evening supplications before the Only One. May the Only One be with you."

After the three replied with the appropriate response, Picaro turned to the center of the room. He rubbed his chin with his left hand and muttered, "Manoah the Lector? I wonder ..."

CHAPTER 25

THE STEADFAST PROMISE OF THE WORD

The third set of knocks on the door of the holy place received an answer. Sunlight immersed the man who answered the door, a powerful man standing six inches taller than Picaro. His short sleeved shirt revealed muscular arms on this man who appeared to be thirty years of age. At the sight of him, Picaro flinched, a reaction from his youthful encounters at the old holy places as well as his years on the battlefield.

The doorkeeper greeted them with a deep, booming voice, "The Only One be with you, my friends. Please enter into one of his holy places."

The three returned his greeting and entered the door giving thanks. Once inside, Picaro told him, "We are looking for Manoah the Lector."

The man replied in an apologetic tone, "Ah, what was I thinking. I should have given you one of my cards."

Picaro continued, "Then you, sir, are Manoah the Lector?"

His voice carried his words, "You need travel no farther. I am Manoah the Lector, guardian and overseer of the holy place here at Oak Fork. How may I serve you?"

Benyonah asked, "Are you permitted to speak with us?"

Manoah the Lector answered with a pleased grin, "Yes, I am permitted."

Picaro studied the guardian's face carefully, his inspection extending a moment beyond what was comfortable for the others. Then he inquired of him, "Are you from the town of Cedarville?"

"Yes."

Picaro responded with roaring laughter and asked another question, "You lived outside the town with your parents and sisters, didn't you?"

"Yes, I did. Who are you?"

"Well, you probably don't remember me. I only spent a few hours with you and your family. We shared a pot of poor-man's stew one evening. I slept in your animal shelter and the next day, I left for the war."

A shocked Manoah the Lector interrupted him and blurted out a booming, "Picaro!" He laughed as the older man's name echoed from the ceiling causing a shiver to ripple down Picaro's neck and back. "Picaro my mighty intercessor! Picaro the Warrior! How wonderful to see you after all these years. I have never forgotten you in either my memories or in my supplications."

Manoah the Lector grabbed Picaro and hugged him, lifting him off the ground in doing so. Picaro felt the strength of youth in the arms of the huge man. He also perceived the loss of power in his own body, the toll taken by both years and war. While being hugged, he had no doubt that, if this mighty man so desired, he could have crushed him to death. Picaro was glad when his feet touched the floor again. He looked at Roja and saw her grinning at him.

"Manoah the Lector, I introduce you to my beloved bride, Roja."

"I am very pleased to meet you, Roja."

She replied, "I am pleased to meet you, too, Guardian Manoah; but I think I would be even more pleased and perhaps even entertained to know more about this intercessor business."

"Me too, mother," added Benyonah with a inquisitive grin.

Manoah the Lector smiled and Picaro said, "What once was for a few seconds will never be again. Manoah the Lector needs no strong-arming assistance from me. Rather, I will look to him for help, knowing that I would get it."

"At your service, my friend," replied Manoah the Lector, "only one day, I will have to give way to this young man."

"I am Benyonah, sir, and I think that with your big voice, you would do a very good job at speaking the *Thrice Calling of the Echo*."

Roja snickered and the men laughed. Manoah the Lector told the boy, "It is true that I am heard and the echoes resound well. However, the power of the rite is neither in the volume of the voice nor the quality of the echo. The ability to bring someone to the Hunter is in the promise of his powerful word and the Hound's pursuit."

The smile on Manoah the Lector's face disappeared as he turned to speak to Benyonah's father, "Picaro, my friend, what is your father's name?"

"Mac. He is one of the reasons I have returned here with my wife and son - to see him, my mother and my brothers and also to visit the area where I was born and raised. Why do you ask?"

The guardian replied in a formal tone, "Please, follow me."

Manoah the Lector led them to the lectern at the front of the holy place. He opened the *Book of the Holy Volume* to a place marked by an envelope.

"Picaro, your father came to this place about six years ago. He showed up one day and left at the end of the service. After that, he came into the holy place every day of the divine service, just as it began and sat in the back. At the end, the old man left before I could speak with him. He talked to no one and gave no opportunity for anyone to speak to him. Nobody knew where he lived. For nearly a year it continued this way. I thought about having someone follow him as he left. It would have been easy since the old man was hunched over, crippled up, and quite frail. However, I decided against having someone follow him. Mac did not appear well in body and his soul may have been troubled. One day Mac remained seated here until everyone left. He gave this letter to me. It was sealed as you see it is today, which means I do not know its contents. He asked me to give it to you should you ever come here. I agreed to do so. Mac told me where he lived and asked me to visit him since he would no longer be able to attend the divine services. Within the month he died. I visited him once a week and was with him when he died. His *Ceremony of Returning the Clay* was four years ago. Here is his letter to you."

A stunned Picaro took the envelope, broke the seal and read the letter.

> Picaro,
> I have not addressed you as son because I gave up my rights as a father when you were very little.
>
> One day when the pain was bad I went into the holy place here and sat down. I heard a message which not only condemned all the things I had done, but also spoke of forgiveness. That word of hope sounded good. After that first service I thought how great it would be if it was meant for me. After coming here and listening for weeks, I began to realize that the Hound who had been chasing me for so many years had tracked me down in my old age. Manoah the Lector spoke of the Hunter's love and I finally realized that it was meant for me too.
>
> I confess that I have been a scoundrel for most of my life and I understand if you hate me for all I did to you, your brothers and your mother. I wish I could take it all back and do it all over again. I can not. I plead the Blood of the Hound and pray that you will read this letter and forgive me.
>
> I thank the Hunter for Manoah the Lector. He brought me the old message, the one of hope. Had I not heard it that first day I stopped at the holy place I might be lost forever.
> Mac

Picaro stood stunned as all the bitterness and hatred and anger of the years drained from him. He handed the letter to Roja and asked her to read it. When she finished, he motioned his wife to give it to Benyonah. She whispered, "What mercy. What grace. Praise be to the Only One," and placed it in her son's hand.

Manoah the Lector watched Benyonah's face as the boy read the letter. When he finished, he looked to his father. Speaking sternly to steady his quivering voice, Picaro said to Benyonah, "Read it again, son." The boy did so and when finished, was told to read it a third time. When he accomplished it, Picaro looked his son in the eye and said, "Don't ever forget what you have just read, my son."

He took the paper from him and gave it to Manoah the Lector.

"A letter like this needs to be read by the guardian of a holy place. Sometimes you may wonder if you are making any difference in the lives of the people who come here. You may wonder if the word that you teach and proclaim accomplishes any purpose. You might even question the wisdom of the Hunter or the pace of the Hound or why the Blessed Wind blows one way or another. Don't change the message. Don't alter the divine service. Tolerate no other ones and repeat, repeat, repeat. Teach the truth over and over. I hope this letter is of help and encouragement to you, knowing that your work of proclaiming the old, life-saving, life-giving message is not in vain."

Manoah the Lector read the letter twice, smiled, choked slightly and put it into his friend's hand. Picaro re-folded the paper, placed it back in the envelope and returned it to the guardian.

The overseer frowned and objected, "This belongs to you, not to me."

He started to give it back to him and Picaro said with conviction, "A letter like this needs to be read by you, and read often to yourself for your encouragement and read to your people for their edification. This letter is for you and for the people who come to this holy place."

Manoah the Lector started to disagree and Picaro raised his hand and stopped him, "Wait, please. Excuse me for speaking so sharply to a faithful overseer and please forgive me for using such commands to one of the Hound's own men. I let you read this so you may know that your work in the past has been helpful. I want you to keep it as a permanent bookmark to remind you of what the people under your care need in the future. If you ever feel tempted to change the message you announce here or tolerate other ones in this holy place, then please examine the contents of this envelope and recall what my father wrote to me about you and the message he heard here. If you are ever pressured to leave out the old hymns or stop singing the *Te Deum*, then I want you to take this letter and read it. In fact, if I may be so bold as to make a request of your time, I ask that every year on the anniversary of Mac's departure from this world and his entry into the Hunter's Den, you read the letter. Manoah the Lector, I am temporally and eternally thankful to the Only One, to the Holy Wind who moved you to remain steadfast and to be instrumental in bringing my father to the Hunter through the merciful pursuit of the Hound."

Manoah the Lector could not speak, but pursed his lips and nodded his head in assent and agreement.

CHAPTER 26

NO RETURNING

Manoah the Lector prevailed upon them to remain with him, his wife, their two children and his mother for two days. His father had been called home to the Hunter's Den. Manoah the Lector had the difficult privilege of presiding over the *Ceremony of Returning the Clay* for his father. Now his mother, son and family lived in the house beside the holy place. The great steel trap, once the focal point in the old farm house outside Cedarville, now occupied the living room wall of the guardian's home.

The visit with Manoah the Lector was filled with stories, particularly ones of a time when Picaro served as a warrior. This interested Roja and Benyonah immensely since Picaro rarely spoke of those stormy years and when doing so had not gone into detail. With great skill, Manoah the Lector summoned those accounts from the old warrior, which served in some cases, as cleansing confessions. In turn, Picaro asked his host about the Cedarville gang, particularly how long before they no longer picked on the now barrel-chested man with bulging forearms. The overseer laughed, recounted several more incidents and told them that one of the gang members was a member under his present guardianship.

The revelation of Manoah the Lector set the tone for Picaro's journey to his homeland, a time of pithy remembrance and sober reflection. His wife and son would be treated to a guided tour and meet many people of his youth. These people told them many stories, but always stories of what once was, of what is no more and what never will be again. Both people and places changed and Picaro discovered his great loss at staying away for too many years.

Traveling to Cedarville, Picaro learned that the shake mill burned fifteen years earlier. Owners built a new mill on the same site. Having told the story of old, Picaro especially wanted to show his family the cave of Paul E. Feemos. After a short search, they discovered that a cheesemaker had constructed a building in front of the cave, the latter now serving as a place to store his cheeses. Roja purchased some of the cheese which tasted sharp.

Woods Town presented itself as a contrast of the old and the new for Picaro. The building guarded by Octavos Theist remained under his bondage. A new holy place had been built across the roadway and the two structures stared at one another in a contentious manner reflecting the creeds confessed within them. The present guardian of the new and true holy place was a quiet, determined man named Barclay the Crucifer. He was permitted to speak and proclaimed the old message of Benel the One with Crushed Heel, who walks and runs once more and forever. With an understanding of the great privilege, this guardian led the assembly in the singing of the *Te Deum*.

Eliza had moved to Woods Town two years earlier and now lived in a small house in the center of the community. The reunion of mother and son became one destined for retelling. In her front yard, Eliza tended to some of her rock roses and potted plants when Picaro opened her gate for his family to enter. She looked up, saw her son and exclaimed, "Picaro!" As they hugged, the negligent son whispered into his mother's ear, "I'm sorry for having been gone so long. You have every right to be angry with me. I'm sorry, mom."

Eliza answered in a gruff manner for all to hear, "Sorry? Angry? What are you talking about? I'm so happy to see you. If you had stayed away a single day more, then I would be angry and you would have a reason for being sorry! Now, tell me who these people are with you, though I am certain I could guess."

"Mom, this is my beloved bride, Roja." They embraced and spoke words of greeting to each other. While keeping one arm around Roja, Eliza turned to the young man in her yard, looked him square in the eye and asked, "What's your name?"

"Benyonah, grandmother."

"Benyonah? Where'd you get a name like that? And don't call me grandmother. You sound like a sissy. You been back east too long, boy? I'm your grandma. You call me grandma."

Picaro smiled. Roja wondered. Benyonah was stunned. "Yes, grandma. My parents gave me my name."

Eliza snapped back, "Your father doesn't look like a yonah at all; maybe an old buzzard, but not a yonah."

A twinkle formed in Benyonah's eye and he wryly suggested, "Grandma, having had the honor of meeting you, it seems quite likely I was named after you."

Eliza turned her head slightly, eyed her grandson, held back a smile and uttered a wary, "Uh-huh. That's not gonna work with me, Benyonah."

Picaro said, "It is obvious to me and really to all, I should think, that the lad is named after my radiant mom and my beloved bride. Don't you think so, grandmother?"

Eliza gave her son a stern look, "Just keep it up, Picaro!"

Picaro grinned. Roja wondered. Benyonah returned to his bewildered state of mind.

"It's good to be home, mom."

"Quit that grinning." She walked to the door, held it open for them and gave directions, "Come inside and sit down." Roja entered just before her husband.

"Picaro, wipe your feet. I don't want mud tracked in all over my house."

"It's been dry and there's no mud around here, mom."

"I don't care. It's good training," she declared, while in her next breath, she hugged her grandson and said, "It's good to see you, Benyonah. Come inside."

Several days later, the three brothers and their families enjoyed a reunion picnic in the backyard of Eliza's place. Raucous laughter erupted as they told story after story. The brothers leveled jovial accusations at one another, especially concerning the muddy footprints discovered on Eliza's ceiling so long ago and the ripe tomato someone put in one of her boots. The brothers erupted in belly-laughs, the wives shook their heads in chagrin and the cousins giggled and gaped in disbelief. All the while, Eliza tapped her foot, squinted her eyes in feigned disgust and bit her top lip with bottom teeth to thwart a smile. The telling of the old tales continued long into the night. Someone built a fire to warm the tellers and the hearers of the stories. Eliza and her family circled the warming atmosphere. The dancing flames ascended to the heavens and flickered yellowish-orange lights to reflect the faces of laughter.

Picaro and his family stayed at Eliza's for several weeks. Picaro yearned for a visit to Upper Woods Camp and The Dell and determined to return before another building fell in ruins or another voice was silenced in death. The family of three made plans to hike to Upper Woods Camp and The Dell. Staying a day or two in each place would be sufficient. Then, rather than returning immediately, they would hike Mount Moriah and stay in a shelter for several days. Araunah, Picaro's old friend, owned a shelter near the timberline they could use. Araunah told them to take time to hike to the Silver Star Waterfall, drink of its crystal water and take the Silver Star plunge in its basin. Roja thought it might be worthwhile to do, but wondered, recalling the wolves. Benyonah considered it a fantastic idea because of both the wolves and the waterfall.

Upper Woods Camp and The Dell disappointed Picaro. A small community replaced and covered all traces of the camp. They had difficulty finding The Dell since the stream had changed channel and the old mill stood in decay, now completely overgrown by the woods. The shack where Picaro once lived had been replaced by a planer shed for hardwood lumber. A large dry kiln extended across the mill yard and changed the orientation of the small settlement. The two old growth fir trees north of the shack, long embedded in Picaro's memory as protection during fir cone fights with his brothers, had fallen or been felled. A healthy stand of second growth fir covered the land that had been an open field to the southwest. Sweeping changes in landscape and structures overshadowed any hints of familiarity. Silently, Picaro led his family through the disoriented setting which, while surreal and disorienting to him, fascinated Roja and Benyonah. When asked questions by his family about buildings, details and features, more often than not, Picaro could only reply, "I really don't know."

    The trio left The Dell early in the morning of the next day and began the long but beautiful hike to Araunah's shelter at the timberline on the mountain. Picaro and his family arrived late in the afternoon. Due much to Roja's insistence, an upper loft was chosen for sleeping. She told them that wolves might come inside the open doorway to the shelter, but they could not climb the archaic ladder to the upper room. An excited Benyonah imagined all manner of critter and criminal using the structure.

    Two days later Picaro and Roja lost their son, their only son, Benyonah whom they loved. His body was never found. Husband and wife returned to Oak Fork. Rather than having the *Ceremony of Returning the Clay,* Manoah the Lector led the assembly in the ancient *Litany of the Hunter's Giving and Taking.*

    "Children, I am not able to continue with the story today. Please leave me until tomorrow."

CHAPTER 27

REBUILDING

"Araunah."

Turning from his supervision of the grinding work, Araunah saw his old friend standing before him and noticed the clenched chin and resolute stance. "You are always welcome here, Picaro. May my mixed tears of sorrow and joy join yours."

"Thank you," Picaro stated with sincerity and set jaw.

"Is there anything I am able to do for you, old friend?"

"Yes, Araunah. I have come to buy the shelter on Mount Moriah. Will you sell it to me?"

In a gracious manner he answered his friend, "No. The shelter is yours."

Picaro continued, "I want to buy it."

His friend explained, "Look, it is yours whether you want to have it permanently as a gift, or to use it whenever you like. I never go there anymore. Really, it is quite a nuisance to me. You would be doing me a favor --"

Picaro interrupted him, "No, but I will surely buy it from you for a price. My wife and I are going to live in it. Tell me how much and I will pay you now. If you do not tell me, then I must leave."

"Please old friend, don't leave. Write down how much you want to pay. I'll write down what I want from you. We will add the two together and divide it in half. That is then the price. Agreed?"

"Agreed."

Every third day Picaro and Roja hiked to town for supplies. Though it took almost an hour longer, they journeyed the longer direct route to Oak Fork rather than getting their supplies from Upper Woods or Woods Town. At noon they stopped to visit Manoah the Lector and his family. Manoah the Lector listened to them and wept with them.

The couple needed many items to repair the shelter and make it ready for the winter -- lumber for the door, a cap for the stove pipe, two chairs, roof patching, bedding, nails, insulation and food supplies. The return hike to the shelter took longer and tired them. On days after the long hike to town and back, the couple worked on the shelter from dawn until dark. On days before the trek to Oak Fork, Roja and Picaro took long walks along the creek trails on the mountain searching for firewood and silently seeking any sign of their son. They always found wood and never discovered anything concerning Benyonah. Whenever the day of the divine service came, either the weekly ones or the great festival days, the couple held hands as they walked to and from the holy place. They never carried supplies back to the shelter on such days.

This schedule of activities kept them busy during the first months after their son's loss. Husband and wife worked and walked until they became physically exhausted at the end of each day. As darkness shrouded the mountain, they climbed the loft and pulled the covers over themselves. Each night they would speak to each other and to the Hunter. Tears flowed freely and often preceded the merciful slumber of the Hound. Physically tired, spiritually challenged and emotionally spent, sleep subdued them quickly and kept them from waking during the night. They always woke before dawn and waited for the sun's impending advent.

In the four months following Benyonah's passing, Picaro and Roja aged a decade. The day's light shortened as the hours of darkness advanced in due season. Their first winter on Mount Moriah was long, bitter and severe, preventing hikes to town for months. The couple filled the days feeding birds, melting snow, making repairs and carrying wood, always doing the chores together, though more often than not, in silent thought and personal meditation. The nights differed as husband and wife were drawn closer together. They talked about what hurt the soul, softly sang the *Te Deum* and the other ancient hymns, quietly discussed the proclamations by Manoah the Lector and prayed for the faithful guardians. They recalled the traditional readings during the winter and cared for one other.

    The first spring arrived and with the new life on Mount Moriah, Roja and Picaro experienced a renewed purpose and rejuvenated spirit. The decision to remain in the area where they lost their son was a silent one, mutually made and never discussed. The rustic shelter would remain their home, a place where the two lovers would grow old together. In the spring, when the runoff melted and flowed, the couple could laugh again. Tears of joy exceeded the ones of grief, though the latter remained close by. Sometimes when the old warrior walked near the refurbished shelter, he heard Roja's hymning within the cabin. He grinned and joined her singing from where he stood. His wife caught the sound of his deep voice and the duet pleased her. Picaro's smile faded whenever he heard the mountain breeze passing through the needle evergreens, a haunting echo blown about by the willing Wind.

CHAPTER 28

AN AUTUMN SUNSET

Thus the seasons cycled for eight years and thus did wife and husband age together as one. The mountain air benefitted both of them and the thinner atmosphere kept the heart beating strongly. Pure air invigorated the lungs with every breath. Fresh, keen air sharpened the mind. Hard work kept them physically tuned.

Nevertheless each summer passed and the appearance of autumnal forces demanded that winter have its place and run its course. Raging winds and heavy snows kept the couple on the mountain in relative inactivity. They awaited the advent of spring and the resurrection of the green. With the snow drifts still deep and the days still short, Picaro and Roja ventured the hike to the holy place. Each long winter exacted a toll on them and impaired their physical ability to recover in the spring. The hike up the mountain from Oak Fort after the divine service became their barometer. At first, they reached full conditioning in early summer. Three years later they were still out of shape at midsummer. In the seventh year, Picaro could not be certain that he regained full vitality until fall.

In the late summer of the eighth year, the differences in conditioning between Picaro and Roja became apparent and significant. Roja could not continue the pace. Arm in arm they hiked, but Roja made frequent stops to rest and catch her breath. Picaro noted this but made no inquiries. Roja only confessed that she felt the years. They both realized that the mountain life might have to end soon.

One holy day, after Manoah the Lector finished the proclamation, Roja leaned against her husband's shoulder and whispered that she would like to stay the night at the guardian's house. Picaro looked puzzled and whispered his assent. He told her they could return to the shelter the following day.

After sleeping later than usual, Roja asked Picaro to send for a body healer. The surprise request startled him since Roja usually doctored herself. A niece of Edith the Quiet came to Roja's side. Manoah the Lector remained outside the room with Picaro, both in silent supplication. After a lengthy examination, the body healer motioned Picaro to come inside. As he entered, he noted that Roja appeared to be sleeping.

The body healer handed Picaro a small, brown sack and said, "Give her this dissolved in hot water. Use a small spoonful. There is enough here for a couple months."

Stunned at the length of time, Picaro asked, "How long will this medicine take to cure her?"

He stared at Roja's closed eyes as the body healer replied, "What I am giving you will calm her, not cure her. Your wife will not get better. Take her home. That is where she wants to be."

Picaro turned instantly to the body healer. Anger and fright mixed to form a distorted countenance. She continued, speaking in a compassionate, undisturbed tone, "Your wife knows. In fact, she told me that she was dying before I began the examination. She knew she was not well and asked me to confirm it."

Without opening her eyes, she called out, "Picaro, please take me home."

"Yes, we will leave quickly and get away from this valley of death. My wife and I do not need this silly business. The air of the mountain and the water of the creek will revitalize her."

"Picaro?"

"Yes, Roja, what is it?"

Her eyes remained closed as she spoke, "Husband, I love you, and right now, I need you very much. I'm not able to hike to the shelter, but I want to return there for what time I have left with you in this life. I'm so sleepy now. But when you are ready, please wake me. Picaro, please do not forget the medicine for pain. I'll need it."

Picaro felt himself to be in a dream as he prepared for the return to the shelter. He rigged a harness for himself between two poles and fashioned a blanketed sling between them for his wife. Roja reclined in the makeshift bed as he started up the mountain trail. He lifted his face unto the hills, a face bearing the marks of worry, strain, anger and pain. His wife's eyes, darkened from the pains of body and soul, gazed backward and down the path already taken.

Time and again, Picaro felt the urge to flee, a natural desire to run away. He believed that in doing so his problems would disappear. He never sought to act on the urge, indeed, he deemed it impossible and thus, he wept. Without Roja, he had no purpose. A second urge, stronger than the first, rose from within, the instinctive impulse to fight. But where was his opponent? Should he pummel the body healer for being the bearer of such awful news? Could he ascend to the heavens and wage war on the Hunter? He sought to compel someone to something but could only wrestle within himself. Thus he cried out in frustration. Harnessed between the two poles of the make-shift litter that bore his wife, Picaro could neither flee nor fight. He pulled.

Each of the next three nights it took to return to the mountain cabin, Picaro built a fire, heated water, made the prescribed tea for his wife and slept beside her in the dark. She slept facing the fire, absorbing heat from the fire and having light when she awoke in the darkness. Picaro lay at her back to warm her and shield her from the dark cold. Thus did she face the light ahead of her and so did he face the darkness in her wake.

On the fourth day they arrived at the shelter in the late afternoon. He left the harness and poles on the ground outside the cabin and carried his frail wife inside. He could not carry her into the loft. Exhausted physically and spent emotionally they slept a few feet inside the front door. They both slept until afternoon the next day, though Roja woke with pain an hour earlier. Hearing the snoring of her husband, she endured the pain for his sake.

Picaro awakened with a start and immediately chastised himself for not giving his wife her medicine. He ached where the harness had pulled against him and continued scolding himself for thinking of these small pains. Getting the fire going and the water boiling seemed to require extra time. Picaro knew his wife was in pain, though she did not admit to it. The midday sun warmed the cabin and Picaro opened the door to let the fresh air replace the atmosphere of death inside the shelter.

As he did, Roja smiled weakly, moistened her lips and spoke faintly, "Husband, look at the ends of the poles on the ground."

"What?"

"Outside. The ends of the poles. See them?"

"Yes, Roja, I see them. What of them, my dear?"

"Do you see how they have dug into the ground and made a rut in the dirt as you drug me up the mountain?"

"Yes."

"Those ruts mark the spot where our life here ends."

Picaro shuddered as he remembered the day he first met her and what she had said as they looked back at the road along the raspberry field. He wept briefly and then pursed his lips saying more to himself than to his wife, "No, I will not speak of this thing now."

"We must speak of it now, Picaro. I have been in intense pain for a long time. It has worsened."

Picaro turned in quick anger, "You did not let me know?"

"You could do nothing then, now it is different. I wanted to spare you the hurt, waiting until I became certain, waiting until I could endure the pain no longer. Picaro, hold me. I hurt."

"The water is hot. Let me fix your tea and I will hold you."

Now his voice was gentle with concern as he sought to ease his wife's pains. His spirit steeped within him and his soul shook as he brewed the medicinal tea and brought it, along with himself, to her. Picaro attempted to feed his wife but she only asked for more brewings and stronger cups of the calming elixir. Night brought many fears to life for both of them. Sleep came in restless spans for Roja, her husband often hearing her mumbling about a boy being swept away from her arms and wolves climbing trees. Picaro's protecting embrace did not keep her sobs from breaking the silent night. These nights disturbed him too. While he brought his wife's life before the Only One in his nocturnal supplications, most often he wrestled within himself and with the Only One. Fear of being alone again rose to high anger at the Hunter.

One morning, her clothes drenched from night sweats, she spoke faintly. "Picaro, take the wagon wheel necklace from me."

Supposing an irritation to her neck, he unfastened the clasp and removed it.

She continued, "Later, please break it in half. You'll know when."

He held her hand and kissed her feverish forehead.

"Picaro, I love you so very much. But it hurts to stay. I can not do this any more. I am weak and the pain is more than I can bear. The tea doesn't help anymore. One thing keeps me here. You. Picaro, will you let me go?"

"He is able to heal you."

"He will."

"You know what I mean. He can do it right now and you will be whole and well. All he has to do is will it."

"Maybe it would not be good for me to be healed like that. Maybe if that happened, I would fall away from the Hunter and the Hound."

"Maybe you wouldn't fall away."

"Neither one of us knows. It's only for him to know and that is why we pray that his will be done."

"He wills this?"

"No, he wills deliverance from this."

"And in so willing, I'm left without you."

"Picaro, have you ever considered that my suffering and dying is necessary for you?"

"And Benyonah?"

"I will soon be with him."

"And me?"

"The Hunter knows all things and does or permits what is going to result in our eternal good. My suffering-"

Picaro stiffened, "Is that what this life comes to? The Hunter causes you to suffer for my benefit. That's a disfigured and cruel test. The Hunter permits you to suffer on my account?"

"Picaro, the Hunter is not the one keeping me here."

Picaro moaned.

Roja did not summon the strength to speak, thus letting her husband think. An hour of turmoil for him and consuming ache for her passed.

He bent down to her face and spoke softly to her. "I love you, Roja. When I met you, my life began and I had purpose. You are the instrument that the Hound used to catch me. I belong to the Hunter because of you."

With quivering lips, she asked again, "Picaro, I can not do this anymore and I can not go. Please, will you let me go?"

"In order to relieve your suffering, I will let you go."

"No, you may not do it for that reason. You must permit me to go because it is okay with you. I can not rest until my death is okay with you. I long to depart and be with the Hunter and the Hound and the Blessed Wind, but I can not leave you until it is okay with you."

He shook as his compassion for Roja struggled with his will that he not be without her. He shuddered at the knowledge that the Hound could heal her with a single thought and despite Picaro's many pleas and petitions, the Hound had not done so. He wrestled with the Only One whose gracious hand gives such blessings like his beloved Roja and whose terrible hand takes her away. For the thousandth time, he fought the temptation to flee and to curse. Responding to a summons that did not originate within him, Picaro spoke resolutely.

"The ruts do end here, Roja, and our life together here may end for now, but it is only interrupted a short time for you, and a bit longer for me. Nevertheless, we will be together later in the Hunter's Den. We belong to Him."

"Will you let me go?"

Picaro wept openly and he shook as he sobbed his one word answer, "Yes."

"Ah yes," she whispered.

"I will be with you later."

As his tears fell on her anemic lips, she parted them and uttered, with the same words, her gratitude to the Only One and to her husband, a silent, "Thank you." She exhaled a peaceful breath and continued, "I love you, my Picaro." She closed her glassy eyes and whispered, "The Only One be with you."

He bent low, kissed her cheek and replied in her ear, "And also with you."

Those were the last words she spoke. The next morning, before the sun rose, while it was still dark, Roja passed away in the arms of her husband. He retrieved something from the table beside him. With a thumb and knuckled finger on each wagon wheel, Picaro broke the necklace in two.

CHAPTER 29

WRESTLING

A small gully, a hundred feet southeast of the shelter, served as the site for Roja's grave. Picaro dug a three foot deep pit in the glacial till. After wrapping her body in the faded purple blanket she had owned since childhood, he used the poles and harness to take her body to the grave. He wept when the last trace of purple disappeared beneath the gray soil. Since he did not have time to cover her body sufficiently in order to prevent disturbance during the night, he remained there. With his blanket wrapped around him to insulate himself from the coldness of the night air and deathly quiet, Picaro sat beside his wife's grave. Numbed, shocked and exhausted, he wept through the night.

Picaro labored another day covering her grave with the gritty soil. For two additional days, he carried larger rocks to cover the resting place of her mortal remains. On the third day, Picaro hiked to the house in Oak Fork where his friend and overseer lived. The guardian conducted the ancient *Litany of the Hunter's Giving and Taking*. Picaro denied Manoah's request for Picaro to remain with him a few days. The old man wanted to return to the shelter to grieve alone on the slopes of Mount Moriah.

As if sensing his numbness and coldness, winter arrived early. Storms processed in cadence against the mountain and dumped heavy snows on its slopes. Icy winds searched for points of entrance in the shelter's roof. Snow drifted to its height. The window on the downhill side of the cabin provided light during the day. The wood supply, stored for years, lasted the winter. The cabin's larder remained full, now drawn upon by only one, a man with little appetite. On a day when the snows fell, the wind blew and only minimal light entered the kitchen area, Picaro sat down with pencil and paper.

Oh, Only One, for Whom eternity
Is but a fleeting instant,
Your time slays me slowly as I await
For my heartbeat's finale
That remains beyond my grasp.
Tantalus and I were sad companions
But he's gone and I'm alone.
You cut my distance to the door in half,
And so distanc'd, I never arrive there.
    Thus, I struggle with You.

    O Grand Hunter, You are the Only One,
    Always reigning securely from Your Den,
    Has Your heart ached at a Loss,
    Of one as close as was mine?
    Of one so a part of me?
    Ah yes, and more, I say,
    Your love sent Him forth to die!

Oh, Only One, in Whose Almighty Word
Is more than omnipotence,
A trace, slight, inkling, smidgen thought of Yours
In one instant could heal her,
Or lesser musing slay me.
Yet neither in Your mercy gave then
Nor pity look on me now,
But rationing strength in declining sums,
And so nourish'd, I never die here.
    Thus, I wrestle with You.

> *O Bloody Hound, You are the Only One,*
> *Running and pursuing at His bidding,*
> *Has death crushed Your heart, Benel,*
> *When snared by the way of life?*
> *When You had no choice but stay?*
> *Ah yes, and more, I say,*
> *Your love bound You caught to die!*

Oh, Only One, in whose presence vastness
Is more present here than everywhere,
Dwelling in the deepest mountain roots and
The darkest caverns of minds,
Dare you be asked to tap me
On stooped shoulder telling me that You AM?
No! For your finger's done so
Summoning once, and now twice, but no more,
And so, untapp'd, I know not now or when.
> *Thus, I contend with You.*

>> *O Blessed Wind, You are the Only One,*
>> *Wafting amidst the befoul'd spirits here,*
>> *Has Your Word blown where You will,*
>> *With one edge to slay flesh'd hearts?*
>> *With another to ease as oil?*
>> *Ah yes, and more, I say,*
>> *Your love bids me die to live!*

Whenever Picaro visited the grave of his beloved bride, he carried one or two large rocks and placed them on the site. He scoured the area upstream and down for rocks to pile, wood to burn and any sign of his son. The former two remained plentiful; the latter he never found. As the years passed, the small gully vanished, being replaced now by a slight mound of rock.

When the season of the year permitted, the weather of the day favored and his health allowed, Picaro hiked to Oak Fork for the divine service at the holy place. He started early, beginning the trek before dawn. He arrived just before the assembly spoke the first "ah yes." The old man sat alone in the back, Manoah the Lector noting it to be the same place occupied by Mac. There Picaro joined the many and sang the *Te Deum Laudamus* with all those assembled in the name of and in the presence of the Only One -- with the guardian, the little ones of all ages, messengers, arch-messengers and all the company of those in the Den including those who from their labors rest.

For the first decade after his wife's death, Picaro made the return journey to the shelter directly after the assembly at the holy place. In the following five years, the hike to and from the holy place rarely happened on the same day. Only on long, warm summer days, when Picaro was in particularly good health, did he do so. He stayed overnight with Manoah the Lector, himself now an older man, and returned to the shelter the following day. The hike to the shelter became more difficult as he lifted up his dimming eyes to those ancient hills. Old legs, though aided by his walking stick, moaned against the load and begged for respite. His weary back hunched over and stooped ever lower under his burdens, both those seen and those unseen. He needed rests along the way and he established favorite spots to take them. One day, in the middle of the afternoon, he paused by a stream and lingered near an old growth fir. The old man took his pencil and wrote.

At the Hour of None

Let the multitudes praise you, Only One,
  O let us sing to You: Hunter, Hound, Blessed Wind.
The little ones of few months praise You,
  Chanting the new song learned so soon.
The son of the dove praises You,
  In the assembly of the holy ones.

The little ones with a score of years, praise You,
   Hymning to the One with crushed heel.
The woman cleaved and cleft praises You,
   In the most high place.
The little ones with bent backs, praise You,
   Blessing Your Name with glorified lips.
The red-haired girl of four would have praised You,
   In blue jeans offering trillium in hand.
The little ones, guarding and overseeing, praise You,
   Honoring Your Name then and now.
All there and I here praising You, O Benel,
   All save that one, who never was,
   For whom my selfish night tears flow.
All there and I here praising You, O Benel,
   Once trapped but now running with Crushed Heel,
   Once more and forever with clear footfalls.
Let the multitudes praise You, Only One,
   O let us sing to You: Hunter, Hound, Blessed Wind.

AH YES! AH YES! AH YES.

Several years later, Picaro knew he could stay no longer. He recalled the cave from years ago, a hole in the mountain visited but once. To remember the way to the cave seemed likely, to attain it a remote possibility. If he made it there, he would die there in the empty, rock room. His bones, discovered by one seeking refuge, might frighten that one away when a stay was needed. He knew what he must do and thus Picaro sang a stanza of an ancient hymn to the One always with him,

>   *'Twas good, Hound, to've been here.*
>   *Yet I may not remain;*
>   *But since Thou calls me leave this mount,*
>   *Walk with me on the plain.*

CHAPTER 30

THE CONTINUING STORY

For the first time since the children arrived grandpa was not at the breakfast table in the morning. They ate quickly and finished their chores without dawdling. Only one more day remained in their summer vacation and they wanted the frail, old man to finish the story. Grandpa entered the house from the back with a small brown sack in one hand.

Gerrie asked, "Grandpa, the old one is late this morning, isn't he?"

"No," he answered, "he's no longer here with us."

The children focused on grandpa as they waited for an explanation.

Mick blurted out, "He's not dead, is he?"

A chorus of voices retorted, "Mick!"

Grandpa chuckled and replied calmly, "No, he's not dead. Last night some people came and took him with them."

The cousins' varied questions came at once, "Who took him?" "Why?" "Where'd they take him?" "Were they bad men?"

"Don't worry, now. He's just fine. Someone learned that he was sleeping in the loft and reported it to the authorities. They telephoned me yesterday about the situation and we made arrangements for him to stay in a nursing home in the northern part of the county."

Ellen queried indignantly, "That's really mean, isn't it?"

Grandpa replied calmly, "It may seem so, but I really believe he wanted to go with them. He did not want to be a burden to us and he could not care for himself. Having him here was no problem." He turned to grandma and asked, "Right?"

"Yes, Manoah. The only thing that bothered me was that we couldn't do more for him. We had plenty of room in the house, but he insisted on living in that old shed and sleeping in the loft."

Grandpa agreed, "His staying here has never been a problem. He is an old friend and I have always enjoyed his company. But to tell you the truth, I am amazed he didn't fall going up and down the loft ladder. So children, I confess to you that I am relieved he's going to be cared for in the nursing home."

Chris sighed and spoke, "But he was so close to the end of the story. He didn't finish it."

Grandpa interjected, "I don't know what your story was all about, but it must have been a good one."

"It was," said Mick with a hint of disappointment.

Kay thought pensively and then responded, "Maybe he didn't finish it because that was as much as he could tell us."

Several asked, "What do you mean?"

"Well, maybe he couldn't finish his story because it isn't done yet."

As the others perceived Kay's comment, grandpa said, "True, possibly very true."

Mick asked quickly, "What about that old dog?"

Grandpa hesitated, "I don't know. With all that took place last night, I really don't know what happened to the dog. I haven't seen him at all this morning. The old dog disappeared."

Mick spoke with concern, "We'll have to watch out for him. Maybe we can take him home. We need to take care of that old hound."

Ellen had been thinking and added aloud, although as if speaking only to herself, "No, I think we've got it backwards."

Putting the wrinkled sack on the table, grandpa spoke, "I checked the loft this morning to see if anything had been left behind. I found this old brown sack by the ladder to the loft. Inside are some things my old friend wanted you to have."

Grandpa took out two small, crudely wrapped packages, one for Chris and the other for Gerrie. The twins quickly unwrapped them. Each received half of the wagon wheel necklace. The chain had been fastened on each half to form a loop large enough to wear as a bracelet. Grandpa dug into the sack again and handed a wadded-up packet to Kay. She unfolded the paper and found a small booklet of handwritten poems. Ellen opened her packet and discovered a necklace with a small object on it. She said it was like the animal trap that Grandpa had hanging on the wall, a small trap used to snare an animal by the leg or foot. Mick opened his package to discover a snuff can. He smiled with a grin of wonder and put it in his pocket.

Grandpa encouraged his grandson, "Open it, Mick, let's see what's inside."

The children replied in unison, "It's empty!"

Attached to each gift was a card written by the old man.

```
I am Picaro from the shelter below
    the empty cave on the side of
            Mount Moriah.
    I may speak to you no more.
        (Please keep this card.)
```

On the other side of the cards, Picaro had penciled a message to the children.

```
His footfalls have echoed the sound,
Of a rogue He pursued and He found,
      You've heard of His glory,
        Now pass on the Story,
Of the Agnus Dei Who is the Hound.
```

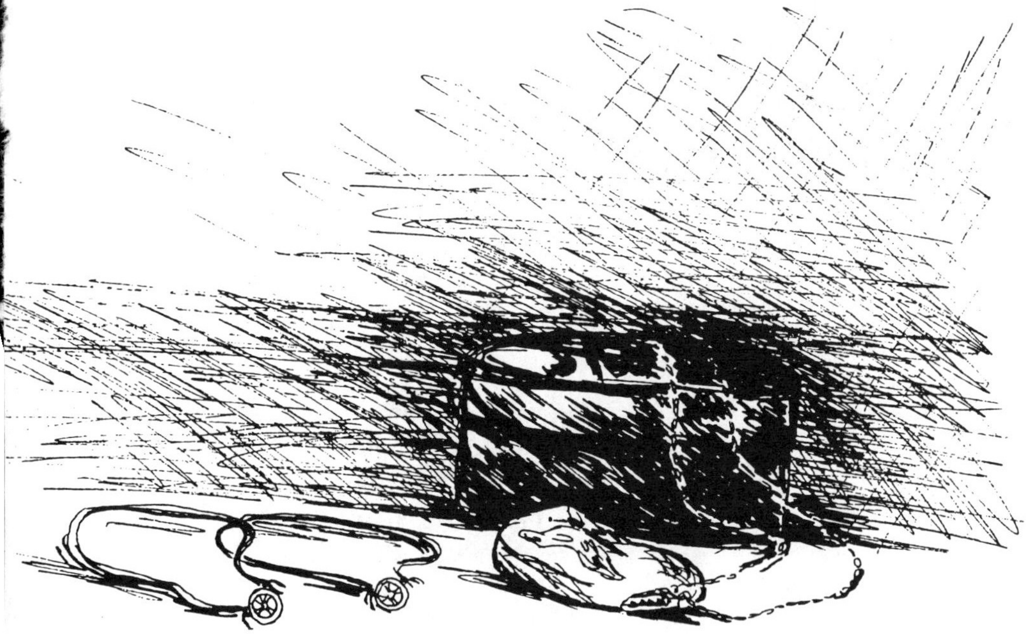

About the artist ...

Anisa L. Baucke has served as teacher at the Evanjelicke Gymnasium (Lutheran High School) in the city of Tisovec of the Slovak Republic where she taught English and Art. She graduated from Concordia University in Seward, Nebraska in 1998 with a Bachelor of Science and Lutheran Teaching Diploma in Art Education K-12 and in Elementary Education. She is an artist in residence in Lincoln, Nebraska.

About the author ...

Michael L. McCoy was raised in the woods near Battle Ground, Washington and worked in his uncle's and grandfather's sawmills at an early age. He served in the U.S. Army Corps of Engineers (1966-1969). He has served as pastor at Our Redeemer Lutheran Church in Emmett, Idaho since 1984. He and his wife, Judy, have three children.

So shall My Word be that goes forth from My mouth;
it shall not return to Me empty,
but it shall accomplish that which I purpose,
and prosper in the thing for which I sent it.

Isaiah 55:11